MEDUSA

Abandon all shame

Lala Idrisse

The characters and events portrayed in this book are fictitious. Any similarity to real persons, living or dead, is coincidental and not intended by the author.

ISBN: 9798846136748

Please take off your clothes, this book is best read naked.

CONTENTS

FOREPLAY: OMEN

Janice drew on her cigarette holder, and due to the poorly fitted filter atop, an almost inaudible, yet enervating whistling sounded as the smoke swirled through the slender ebony shaft. Jana raised her eyes. She had not prohibited smoking in the great conference room, yet they all knew she disapproved. Janice also looked awkward with the nearly forearm-long, raven-colored cigarette holder. This antiquated accessory called for a pearl necklace, a wide-brimmed hat, leather gloves, and the famed little black dress. Janice was wearing a flaming red costume and a white blouse with a girly lace collar, as if a dummy had been advised to dress business-like for this particular gathering. Her light brown hair lay over her shoulders and her feet were in stilettos, scarlet as the dress, whose sex appeal clashed with the pseudo-business nature of the rest of her outfit.

Jana glanced at the wall at the far end of the room. A good-looking woman smiled down at her from an enormous flatscreen. "The hospitality expo has been good for me," she said with a strong African accent. Jana smiled.

"That's wonderful, Shauna. Unfortunately, I'm not convinced that a convention would help my establishment."

Shauna laughed. "Why not, girl? Jus' go there and tell 'em to come!"

Jana smirked along with the sympathetic laughter of the other ladies. "I don't think our target audience attends the kinds of conventions that let our business exhibit."

"What about a convention aimed at performers, not the consumer?" purred Tatjana, a young lady with dark hair and tanned skin. Her body was lean, even muscular, but when she smiled, her lips dug two sweet, deep wrinkles into her soft cheeks. The conference room murmured in approval.

Jana shook her head. "They wouldn't come here. Why would they?"

Janice nodded tentatively. "I say newspaper ads."

Jana mimicked the nod and agreed with the somewhat tepid measure. "Classic advertising it is, then?"

The meeting members fell embarrassingly silent, thereby giving a loud answer.

"A podcast," Carlotta, the youngest among them, said in a soft voice. Janice hummed her annoyance. Jana was interested. Shauna nodded from the screen with a grin and looked into the lower left corner of the pixelated rectangle.

"Keep talking, dear…" Jana demanded sweetly, and someone giggled.

Carlotta cleared her throat. "Yeah… a podcast." She was already blushing. "We could talk about the house and the things we do. Forty-five-minute episodes, maybe? We talk about different practices, how to do them without risk of injury, where we get the clients, who we are, how we got here."

"Talk show without the show," Janice clucked, and ash fell from the tip of her cigarette onto the leather-covered conference table. Jana inhaled sharply. Janice noticed and snapped her finger. A man stepped to her side, hands clasped behind his back. She gestured absently at the ashes and turned back toward Carlotta. The man bent over the table and licked up the ashes officiously.

Carlotta continued, "And, at the end of each episode, we directly address the listeners and ask them to apply if they think they have what it takes."

"Too broad an audience," another lady, Selina, remarked, tossing her curly black mane over her shoulder. "But this is totally going in the right direction." Selina was only slightly older than Carlotta and wore her business attire with the integrity Janice wished she exuded. "The podcast is something Tom, Dick, and Harry can find, but I don't want Tom, Dick, and Harry to apply here." She sat back and stretched her legs out under the table, looking up at the ceiling. "We need something exactly like this, but *extremely* customized. We need to make sure the right people find it."

Jana nodded and made a note. The quiet scratching of her black fountain pen did not go unnoticed.

"Decision made. Jana's already writing," Tatjana said, and the attendees laughed.

Jana winked at her. "Please, don't let me influence your brainstorming. All ideas are good ideas."

"Brainstorming is totally innocuous, but sounds so frivolous," Janice said, laughing gutturally. "You'd have to turn that into a play in a tongue-in-cheek way." A few smiled, agreeing with her. Jana barely contained an eyeroll.

Selina leaned forward again and took her feet off the back of the man lying beneath her section of the conference table. "We did rule out a website, didn't we?"

Jana nodded. "I don't want that anymore since… back then. We had hundreds of applicants within days, flooding the inbox with bad English, price negotiations, nudes, and silly inquiries about whether we were doing this or that for this or that amount of money."

The ladies groaned in annoyance.

"When was that?" Carlotta asked quietly.

Jana sighed. "A good eight years ago."

The young woman smiled cautiously. "Nowadays, they

have specialists who can design a page so that only very specific people will find it – if they've entered exactly the right search terms beforehand." Seventeen beautiful heads turned toward Carlotta, and the petite figure almost sank into the austere reclining chair. "Oops," she chirped nervously, and the ladies laughed, but not in a malicious way.

Jana tilted her head affectionately at the sight of her youngest employee taking the spotlight. "Honey, please explain what you mean."

Carlotta's blonde bob cut swayed cautiously. "It's called search engine optimization. You can make your website come up very high in search results for your preferred search term – given you're doing it correctly. It's technically free – you just have to pay the person who defines the search terms. And who, of course," she added, "writes and designs the actual web page so that it's easy to find and looks nice."

"Rings a bell," Tatjana said. "Back in my studio days, I had a client tell me that my website – because I had so much about leather, bridles, whips, and boots on it – was a top search result for 'dressage' in Brightley Cove." The ladies burst out laughing.

CHAPTER 1: CONTENT CONSENT

Hunched over an outrageously expensive salad bowl, Peter Wartmann opened the most important email of his life and sucked a piece of spinach out of his teeth, chewing loudly thereby.

His colleague snorted without turning away from her screen. "Eat up, Pete."

He ducked his head guiltily. "Sorry."

Peter was filling in for the deputy agency manager, so for the past week, he'd been receiving emails from prospects and first-time clients via the "Any questions? Contact your web specialist here!" button on their agency's website. Usually, his employer, an agency called "Web Specialists," handled small businesses and middle-market companies looking to build their first website or improve their search engine rankings. He made sure that the local carpentry shop ranked #1 in search results when someone typed "carpentry" in *city name* or "furniture" in *city name* in the search box.

The subject of the most important email of his life, which was far too long and exceeded the maximum width of the text field, read: "Request: Search engine optimization for extremely specific target group. Open."

He puffed his cheeks and slowly released the air. Someone had probably experienced poor customer service at another agency and was now making sure the recipient was put on notice via this brusque little imperative. Peter read the email content and didn't notice that he had stopped eating his extremely small, extremely hip, and extremely pricey downtown salad.

Dear Sir or Madam,

We are a small company that has been extremely successful in acquiring and training servants for sophisticated ladies over the past 24 years. Our main focus lies in physical and intellectual education as well as in the teaching of manners and the establishment of sexual expertise in numerous areas. We provide our clients and their property with discretion, a great deal of experience, and empathy.

Our institution is renowned for the exceptional quality of its products and the careful selection of those of the male sex who are eligible for training. We are concerned about the social developments of our time and wish to counteract the dwindling of resources which we perceive by means of a professional internet presence.

We would like to request a quote for the creation of an appealing, search-engine-optimized website for our company. If you have any questions, please do not hesitate to contact us. We are aware of the unique nature of our requirements.

Yours sincerely,

The ladies of the house

Peter gulped.

His colleague looked up from behind her snow-white screen. "Everything all right?"

He shook his head cautiously. "Sandra, I think this is an inquiry from a high-class brothel."

She snorted. "You're shitting me."

He stared at the screen. "Yes, it is. They want a website and SEO. They describe what they do, and it reads like a mixture of call-boy academy and dominatrix venue."

Sandra rose to her feet with a smirk. "Let me see!" She made her way behind Peter's office chair and propped a hand on the back of his seat. Her mouth moved silently as she read. Some of the most important terms escaped her lips in a whisper, "Establishment of sexual expertise… Clients and their property… Selection of those eligible for training…" She shook her head in amazement. "Signed, the ladies of the house."

Peter grinned. "A brothel that's so fancy, it doesn't call itself a brothel?"

Sandra laughed. "Or it's a troll," she decided, nodding toward the taskbar of Peter's desktop. "Get your snipping tool out, screenshot that thing, and off to Twitter with it. This is so weird, it's awesome again. We'll write a funny line about it. Something like: 'The crisis also affects companies that you don't think about right away.' Frank will figure out something witty."

Peter grumbled uncertainly, "And if it's not a troll and they feel offended?"

She rolled her eyes. "Yeah. We call or write back before we do something like that, I guess. You can wait for Christian to return, so he can do it and suck up the inevitable 'You got pranked, bro! Subscribe to my shitty YouTube channel!'"

The silent insinuation that he didn't have the balls to write back annoyed Peter, and he stirred his salad bowl uncertainly.

Selina wielded the slender silver pen with the confident elegance of a huntress trotting leisurely after a wounded, slowly diminishing prey. The slave's limbs jerked anxiously, but that would subside. Jana's house dispensed with the oppressive aesthetics of classic sadomasochism, so the male in front of Selina was not wriggling on an intimidating, spikey, X-shaped cross, but rather on two simple ropes attached to the salon's reinforced lamp hilts. A bulky secretaire with numerous drawers, shelves, and charmingly enameled compartments for writing utensils occupied half of the western wall, and a fire burned under the mantel. Books upon books filled dark wooden shelves.

It would have been easy to place antique-looking panels or even fake books on the shelves, giving the impression of ancient tomes, but Jana didn't like gimmicks and deception, so more modern, ordinary books stood on the shelves. The colorful spine bindings and varying book sizes robbed the salon of a little bit of its Victorian grandeur, but that didn't bother the mistress of the house as much as pretend antiquity would have. Tall transom windows let in plenty of light, and a gardener beckoned Jana from outside when she spotted her employer passing by.

The slave screamed.

Selina slapped him across the face and hissed sharply, "I thought you were a big boy, number Seventeen?"

Sobbing.

Jana could not see Seventeen as Selina stood in front of the slave and fiddled with his abdomen. Only his arms, stretched out wide, protruded above the black-haired woman's shoulders. "You've got curves in all the right places," Jana commented on the sight of Selina's bent-over behind.

Selina laughed and her black curls tossed around her neck. "Thank you, my dear."

Jana sat on a chair with her legs comfortably crossed, typing into her smartphone. She had sent the appointments for next week to her ladies and, of course, Janice had to ask how to save the appointments to her own calendar. Jana didn't use her often, but she liked Janice despite her quirks and the occasional faux pas she committed. The ropes crunched as the slave wriggled in panic and screamed again. After enjoying the sound of another of Selina's slaps, Jana decided not to be angry with Janice. She believed Janice could sense her occasional reluctance, which made Jana uncomfortable and upset the most experienced of the ladies of her house.

"Tap and hold the icon briefly and then select 'add' when the little text appears," she explained to Janice via text. "Then your phone will vibrate and tell you it has saved the new appointments."

Janice's response took time. She typed slowly. "Thanks, worked."

Jana responded, "Love you, my most tech-savvy noodle."

Janice replied with a series of affectionate emojis.

"Ta-da!" Selina sang and stepped aside. The tip of a smooth, slender metal rod protruded from the slave's glans. After being inserted with copious amounts of lubricant, the slim implement was held in a horizontal position by his erection's tight grip. The metal stretched his seminal canal, causing as much pain as pleasure. The result was a man staring at his abdomen in shock, not knowing whether to scream or moan. The compromise of both seemed to be an undignified whimper.

Jana nodded appreciatively. "You're making progress, Seventeen."

The slave nodded with a sob, "Thank you, Lady Jana." His voice sounded muffled because Selina had tied one of her high heels in front of his nose with a thin leather strap. He breathed her in.

Selina patted his belly. "Your future owner will be pleased, darling."

A snort and a distinct nod. "Thank you, Lady Selina. I am so gratefuu—aaah!"

She had turned the small protruding part of the shimmering metal device that bore the crude name *penis plug* a few degrees. As if adjusting the volume on a stereo, she let the slave scream up and down a scale that went through marrow and bone. The ladies laughed out loud at this hilarious detail, before Selina removed the penis plug with tantalizing, yet necessary, slowness. She looked deep into the eyes of the slave, who had the heel of her shoe sticking out of his face like a pointed, overtly long nose, while doing so. He held her intense gaze through glazed eyes. She smiled tenderly. "That's my big boy."

Jana's smartphone vibrated, and she pressed a button to put it on standby and read the message on the lock screen. She had expected a question from the ladies about the appointments but had discovered other, more exciting words: "RE: request: search engine opti—" The rest was cut off by the message's small space. With a thievish grin, she opened the email.

Dear Ladies of the House,

Thank you for your inquiry regarding the design and optimization of your website. Unfortunately, I could not find any company address or other references to existing websites of your business in your email. The nature of your query seems truly unusual. I would be delighted to schedule a meeting with you.

Yours sincerely,

Peter Wartmann

M. Sc. SEO & Analytics

"Ooh," Jana sang conspiratorially, holding the screen to Selina's face. "A 'Master of Science' has replied to our email."

Selina clapped her hands excitedly, forgetting to pull the plug further out of the slave's penis. "What's his name?" Jana held up the smartphone again. "Peter Wartmann," she read, and the ladies looked at each other, eyebrows raised in amusement.

"Sounds jagged and unfunny," Selina judged.

Jana pursed her lips and nodded. "Analytics… I bet it's a chubby nerd in a corduroy suit." Her friend smiled broadly and raised a finger. "No, it sounds like a young man with glasses, good manners, and the early signs of a nerd-neck."

The two ladies laughed.

"You're so awful, Selina!"

Peter didn't tell his girlfriend about the special inquiry he had received and responded to today. Luisa reacted badly to such things. Not that there had been such incidents in the past, but any harmless innuendo, any tongue-in-cheek humor was wasted on her. Luisa could guffaw at political satire, at "Subscribe to my channel!" bellowing pranksters on the Internet, at non-obscene standup comedy, and at the antics of her single girlfriends who made a running gag out of the penis size of their one-night stands. He would have loved to tell her about the ladies of the house who had asked for a website for some sort of fancy slave academy and laughed along with her at the idea, which was most certainly a joke. She had just been chuckling at a remark made by one of her colleagues, and he reciprocated her smile tormentedly.

"When will Christian be back?" Luisa asked absently as she put her plate in the dishwasher.

Peter grumbled for a moment and recalled the date. "On the 26th, still a good week-and-a-half to go."

She nodded. "Are you doing okay with his inbox?"

Again he grumbled. What a setup. He should tell her – in an amused, flat tone. She'd laugh at it too, right? "I never really believed him," he said, deciding not to tell her about the ladies. "But most requests are really just crap. Sure, people don't know much about it, and it's nice that even the mom-and-pop shop in Boulder has realized the Internet is important, but they have outlandish ideas about it."

Luisa was all too familiar with Peter's complaints about nonsensical demands. "Another one who wants his farm store to rank higher than an entire grocery chain?"

Peter snorted as he recalled the ranting farmer who thought a website would automatically launch him to the top of the turbo-capitalist organic food chain. "This stuff occurs more often than I thought, honestly," he admitted, and they exchanged smirks as they sat down on the couch.

"Can you delegate some jobs to Sandra?"

Peter was silent for a moment, which earned him a nudge in the ribs.

"Hey," she breathed seriously, betraying the truth of her question.

He shook his head. "Not really. She's good but can only analyze. I can run the analysis, define search terms, and even write it all up for you in a presentable form and pick out some pretty pictures." He had intentionally talked smack about Sandra. His girlfriend didn't like his female coworkers. She had no reason not to – no female colleague would ever be attracted to Peter, of all people, thanks to his too wiry figure, his nose that somehow sat too high, and his tendency to keep his head down. He glanced at his girlfriend for a moment. She was looking at the TV, relaxed, reassured that Peter wouldn't give any tasks to Sandra and thus wasn't in danger of talking to his female coworker.

The morning brought exciting news. The ladies of the house had replied to his email and still sounded like they did in their first inquiry. Either this was an extraordinarily dedicated troll, or the request was genuine.

Dear Mr. Wartmann,

Thank you very much for your reply. We do not have a website to show you, and we keep the address of our company a secret to outsiders. This shall not get in the way of your work. Our prior knowledge is limited – we would be very happy to schedule a meeting with you. We contacted Web Specialists because your agency is located close to our company, so don't worry – you won't have to travel for several days. A location will be sent to the mobile number at the bottom of your email at 2 p.m. in four days.

The ladies of the house

Peter answered the email and kindly confirmed. Bold of them to simply assume he had no other appointment at said time.

"Ha! See?" teased Tatjana, winking at Jana. "The appointment thing totally worked out."

Jana sighed defeatedly and put her smartphone into a bite-proof leather case, which she, in turn, put into the mouth of the slave walking on her leash. Tatjana, Jana, and Muffin were walking the spacious grounds of the house, enjoying the warm rays of the sun. Muffin was a slave who enjoyed quiet moments full of erotic abandon. Jana's hand routinely guided the champagne-colored leash. Little Carlotta had difficulties dealing with him because he didn't buy the petite blonde's strictness, and her falsetto voice was probably more amusing than dominant when she peeped orders.

Tatjana grinned. "We shouldn't act like petitioners." She had justified her own idea with the wording of the proposed appointment.

Jana agreed. "Nevertheless, we are making a legally binding deal. I'd like to appear serious."

"You aow abfulutely feriouf!" Muffin assured her with the leather case between his lips.

Jana patted his head. "Thank you, sweetie. However, you still won't be allowed an orgasm."

Muffin nodded understandingly, but his eyes made clear that he had not uttered those words in hopes of earning a sexual climax.

Tatjana paid no attention to him. "Concerns?"

Her employer wasn't sure. "Not about the actual business, but about its implications."

Tatjana remained silent, demanding a clearer explanation.

"I dug into this SEO," Jana said, "last night after the theater." The theater was an infrequent show in which particularly well-behaved slaves performed an ever-changing, well-rehearsed play before the assembled residents of the house. It was akin to a study, vivid paintings of the nude, entwined bodies creating sighing works of art. "We have to put a lot of thought into the terms that we use. It has to be… stylish," she said, unsatisfied with her own description.

Tatjana believed she understood. "Like in the email. 'Servants' instead of slaves. 'Clients' instead of dominatrixes, and so on."

Jana shook her head. "No. Much more… elevated."

Tatjana sighed. "The Specialist will know what to do."

Jana was hoping. Muffin didn't crawl on the harsh, cobbled path, but slightly staggered behind them on the lawn. The ladies were no inhuman sadists, after all. They had reached the far edge of the large eight the path described in the house's garden and paused. A weeping willow lowered its long branches into a deep, almost black pond. Jana would have liked swans to settle there, but they needed a lot of water to land and take off. Trimming a healthy animal's flying feathers just to be able to keep it in her yard for aesthetic reasons didn't fit into the philosophy of the house or of Jana's. Muffin caught up and knelt beside her. Jana put a hand on his mess of black hair and stroked it absently. He tilted his head and leaned gently against her hip. She allowed it. Tatjana glanced at his crotch. He was wearing a white plastic appliance between his legs that prevented erection and any sexual stimulation. At the same time, the chastity device nudged his testicles upward, literally presenting them under the penis cage. Like two small, plump balls, they bulged out from under the plastic.

"How long have you been without release, muffin?" Tatjana asked.

"F-free momphs," he mumbled round the case in his mouth.

Jana nodded in commendation. "We're battling addiction with fervor."

Tatjana hummed sweetly and pursed her lips. "Brave little doggie." She stretched out a leg. "Take off my shoe." Muffin untied the laces of the red sneaker with tender reverence. Tatjana slowly slipped out of the shoe, literally gliding out of the opening. She wore small, gray sports socks that ended below her ankle. Jana observed the sweet ritual. "The sock," Tatjana commanded, and Muffin respectfully grasped the soft fabric to pull it off her petite foot. Tatjana was well toned. Jana admired the strands of muscle visible beneath her black leggings as she balanced for a moment while Muffin removed her sock. She stepped into the soft grass, and Muffin repeated the ceremony on her other foot. "Put one sock in the shoes," she said, and Muffin followed through.

Jana took the smartphone from his mouth. Tatjana untied the leash from his neck and passed it to Jana. "Ya wanna play, Muffin? Yes?"

He nodded decisively. The man, who used to be called Mustafa, now Muffin, greedily opened his mouth to be allowed to transport Tatjana's remaining sock in it. Tatjana and Muffin stepped out onto the lawn. Jana, in her chic pumps and flowery little dress, remained on the path and looked at the two of them with an almost motherly gaze, rolling the champagne-colored leash up and down in her hands.

Tatjana took the sock from Muffin's mouth, praised the surprising dryness of the fabric, and tossed it. The little sock obviously didn't fly very far, but it was enough to make Muffin crawl after it and retrieve. Tatjana laughed at the sight of the penis cage bobbing back and forth between his legs. Muffin gathered the sock from the grass with his mouth and returned it, grinning proudly. Tatjana smirked. "Such a good boy!" She squeezed the sock against his nose. "Enjoy it." He inhaled deeply, sighed, and cradled his head gratefully on his shoulders, following her rubbing, almost lathering motions. The two women exchanged a cheeky look. Muffin moaned and took a deep breath. Tatjana tossed the sock a second time. "We'll do this until you can identify my socks in a full basket of laundry and distinguish the sport I participated in beforehand based on the taste."

Jana snorted. She loved Tatjana's foul mouth. Muffin's sock fell from his lips in delight at this idea, spoken as a threat, and both women laughed at his enthusiastic facial expression.

"Petie's going to a broooothel," Cathrine announced in the rhythm of a children's rhyme and spread her arms in the corridor between cubicles. The colleagues by the coffee machine roared, and Peter laughed loudly with them.

"Yeah, considering how stressful working here can be," he proposed sarcastically, "You know how we all have to vent a little bit outside our relationships every now and then."

Before Peter could even finish the sentence, his female colleagues put their hands on their hips in mock indignation. " Excuse me?! Hello?"

The men laughed. "Awesome client, Pete."

He shook his head humbly. "I'm still expecting someone to jump out of the bushes at the appointment and shout 'It's a prank, bro!'"

Cathrine, a bubbly, sympathetic woman with horn-rimmed glasses and a short, platinum-blonde haircut, winked. "I don't think so. I've seen the emails."

Peter reached for one of the empty mugs on the shelf while the other coffee drinkers retreated to their offices. "They've got literally nothing so far – zero, zilch, nada," he explained. "Not even a *bad* website. A playground to frolic in, sure – not a great area of business, though."

"Well, your 'ladies of the house,'" Cathrine said it like the name of a movie villain and added comic laughter, "certainly won't make the references on our homepage. Still..." – she looked around for a moment – "this is absolutely awesome."

He laughed and selected a macchiato before agreeing, "It is definitely exciting."

Cathrine gave him a playful punch. "Jeez! Did you even read the emails? This isn't about a little page for the local fetish club. It's hot shit."

He rolled his eyes at Cathrine's choice of words. "Yeah, you're right. But what's to come of it? I know such s—" They both laughed abruptly at what phrase almost escaped

Peter. "I can *imagine* how such pages look," he salvaged, enjoying the wonderfully frivolous moment he was sharing with this smart, charming woman who was not looking for a deeper sexual meaning behind every flirtatious phrase and scandalizing it. He enumerated, "A big ol' 'adults only' warning pop-up at the beginning, a 'Welcome to our site' banner with a big picture of some sexy ladies, two or three detail pages with more pictures and a few – how to call it – exercises? Games? And then a few pictures of the equipment used to maltreat the gentlemen: That's what such sites look like."

Cathrine grinned wryly. "'Maltreat.' Do you know you talk differently when you're emotionally invested?"

He raised an eyebrow.

She continued, "You're in the right place. Read through the emails again, Peter. These women don't want a 'Welcome, dear client! A whipping will cost you a hundred bucks per hour' type of site."

"He'll define keywords," Carlotta said, as she stretched out on the couch of her spacious apartment in one of the house's towers. Jana sat down across from her. The soft material sighed under her weight. Of all the ladies, Carlotta knew her way around the Internet the best, even if Jana considered herself a firm navigator of the World Wide Web. The sassy blonde glanced briefly at the ceiling. "If he's good, we'll be allowed to have a say in it. It's about the most important terms we want to be found by."

Jana was happy to find an entry point into this topic. She asked, "In the sense of: if we put *banana* on the website, anyone who types in banana will find us?"

Carlotta grinned and reached for her cocktail glass. The pillow beneath her shifted to cushion her movement. Jana stroked the couch that had been formed by two men, with great muscular effort, across the chest. "Sort of, yeah. You notice when you search for something yourself that the search engine's gotten smarter and smarter in the last few years."

Jana tilted her head uncertainly. Carlotta laughed softly and put her glass back on the rear of a third man, who was serving as her table. A fourth man stood at attention in the corner, holding a massive, baroque lamp over them. Two undressed women, their arms and legs cleverly interlocked, formed a chaise longue in front of the fireplace, a place where Carlotta liked to read. She winked at her boss. "The algorithm reads by itself now. You won't be found if your address is 'buy bananas now dot com' but the content of your website is about exotic cars."

Jana nodded and voiced the mental note she was making, "The address has to speak for itself, too."

Carlotta nodded considerately. "However, that exhausts my knowledge."

Jana smirked. "You know more than all of us put together, dear."

Carlotta sighed. "I would do anything to help you, Jana." She straightened up, turned, and put her bare feet into the mouth of the slave serving as her table. Carlotta had lovely, slender little toes. Her nails were a little arched, a characteristic some women detested having, but it suited her. The slave sighed with gratitude and sucked eagerly. Carlotta loved colors that were on the brink of slipping into pastel but did not. Her nail polish was a Caribbean turquoise. Her servants wore slim panties and bikini tops in warm tones from which their exceptionally large cocks and breasts constantly threatened to spill out. Inside her quarters, Carlotta herself wore no clothing at all. Two small, adorable breasts rested against her chest; she had a large round navel and slender legs. The couch slaves' cocks were constantly erect from Carlotta's incessant touching. She liked to sit on one of them when she spent time at her gaming console. Today, the table slave seemed to be in particular favor. She smiled down at him and slowly pushed her toes, one by one, into his mouth. "The dust," she purred, and his tongue slid into the spaces between her toes.

Jana watched for a while as the beautiful Carlotta's little feet underwent an intense cleaning in the mouth of the slave kneeling on all fours. It was a sloppy procedure. She absently dipped her toes in his mouth, wiped saliva on his cheek, and occasionally glanced at her feet to assess the cleanliness. "Helps when you have cold feet, too," she said at one point, and Jana playfully poked her side. Her half of the human couch had a rock-hard erection sticking up between Jana and Carlotta's thighs. The tether of a game console's wireless controller hung from it. Carlotta had passed the time with it before Jana arrived. She registered her boss' look and unwound the strap. "You wanna? He's so happy whenever anyone needs him, because I usually sit on this side here."

Jana shook her head. "Thanks, love. I'm sure he would more than satisfy me, but I'm not in the mood."

The blonde winked. "He'll relax you."

"I'll get back to you on that when I clear my head."

Luisa didn't apologize for letting Peter wait. She had never done that, not even in the beginning. He forgave her. Peter had had neither too little nor particularly much success with women but rather had a typical youth, with three real relationships lasting several years and two that he dismissed as crushes. College had been another matter. Luisa and her almost outrageous selfishness in romantic things had made his passion burn hotter than any before. She made him feel like he was about to make a conquest. Her refusal, her delaying of intimacy, made her valuable. He wanted to climb a mountain at the top of which waited her real, genuine, uninhibited affection. Each romantic evening carried him higher; each hurdle overcome laid a foundation in her pretty head on which he could build a house for them both. Each milestone was hard-won in his relationship with Luisa. The first time he had sex with her had cost breaking off contact with Jamie, one of his football friends from high school. The price for moving in together in his apartment had been a viciously worded disinvitation to his dearest female college friend from an alumni reunion. Luisa's love had grown with his sacrifices, and he burned for that feeling. He had made the greatest sacrifice for her respect toward his erotic preference: He loved her feet. Her soft toes, the fragrant sole, and the wonderfully curved arch of her foot. His life's planning had been the sacrifice for having a girlfriend who allowed his fetish. He loved her for her tender disregard for "that sexual *thing* you have." The expensive apartment in an interchangeable downtown, four hours from home, had been the price. The move, the change in his life plans, the switch to a smaller agency where he had to drag the eager, but slow, Sandra along, had been the price of his sexuality. So Luisa often – not always – let him have his way when he greedily licked the soles of her feet to keep up his erection, never contorting her face right in front of him when he playfully hinted at a bite on her big toe. When he was annoyed with her, he called her "princess" in the now rare phone calls with his old friends, because she allowed herself to do things for which she would scold him.

When Luisa finally walked out the door and said goodbye to her coworker Paul with a hug, Peter rolled down the car window, waved, and teasingly shouted, "Hey buddy, hands off my girlfriend!"

Paul laughed and waved back. "If you don't watch out, Peter, I'll steal her someday."

Peter winked. "You and what army, massage slut?"

Paul flashed him a friendly raised middle finger.

"Sorry, office wagey."

Luisa got in and gave him an incensed look. "I know men can really bitch at each other," she commented on the exchange. "But don't drag my job into it. We sell medical equipment and supplements that are also used by therapists. Paul is definitely not a massage slut"

Grinning, Peter drove off. "Sorry, honey. He's likable, but his hugs just take that one quarter of a second too long – the difference between 'See you tomorrow, fellow colleague' and 'Heyyy.'"

She snorted but couldn't hide her satisfaction at his jealousy. "Pedant."

He shrugged. "How was your day besides that?"

She buckled her seatbelt. "We're still stocking up on peels. The Chinese are buying it in spades at the moment."

He remembered this story. "Did you find out why?"

She just snorted again and typed a message into her smartphone. "It's Anna's birthday," she announced instead of answering his question.

He knew she liked it when he started imagining things without thinking too much about the friend in question, so he nodded and put on his blinker, watching a black compact that didn't seem sure of which lane to take. "I said happy birthday on her post today." He knew Luisa had seen his congratulations.

She nodded. "She wanted to party, but midweek is really dumb."

"If she does have a party later on, what should we get her?" Peter knew what to buy for Luisa's friend Anna. He memorized things she said about her friends and stored them away to be able to impress her with them later. These memories, however, had to be casually uttered in order to maintain the appearance of mere caring. "Wasn't there talk about too many bottles of wine that she keeps getting as gifts? I think you mentioned that at one point."

Luisa laughed chuckling and lowered the phone. "Right! The wine *rack*," she elongated the last word suggestively, making it clear to him that she found the harmless double entendre incredibly funny as long as she and her friends were the originators of the joke.

Jana asked Janice to make sure that the servants of the house were not wandering the corridors naked at the time of her appointment with Mr. Wartmann. Permanent nudity was perfectly normal for many servants in the house, but visitors were spared the sight – it was lust, not perversion, that reigned here. Janice was none other than Jana's Domina. Not in the modern, sexually charged, leather-and-chains sense, but quite ancient: Domina, the wise, orderly spirit of the *domus*, the house in ancient Rome, the pure, loving force that kept things in order with as much rigor as tenderness. Janice was born for the task. Where her heels clacked across the parquet, silence reigned; where her hand guided, chores were completed efficiently.

Janice's smile eclipsed the sly grin of the Nemesis who gazed through poison green eyes in an oil painting that had been lost, returned, seemingly cursed, sold and bought back. It hung threateningly above the domina's desk. Jana was envious of Janice's painting. No, she envied Janice for the idea of the painting. The goddess held an hourglass and a sword in her hands. A criminal, the victim of his violent act at his feet, was turned away from her glow in shame. Jana had not quite manage to put her thoughts into words, but "glow" was not properly expressed. Nemesis did not radiate light but rather absorbed it. The guilt of the criminal beneath her shone like a bonfire. She had merely followed the vile glare of his deed and appeared to judge him. The art trader back then dared to explain to the six prima donnas walking up and down his gallery that she was the goddess of justice. But Nemesis brought revenge, not justice. Jana smiled thinly. Of the six buyers from that time, only three were still here: Janice, Selina, and herself.

Janice raised her gaze. "The longer you stare," she said, "the harder you swing the whip afterward. Own observation."

Jana grinned. "Never." Her oldest and most difficult friend opened her hands in an inviting gesture.

"You're free to try, boss." She pointed to a slave whose hands were stuck in two openings in the wall. Red lines stretched across his back. He stood alone in Janice's large office, staring at the wall as she made lists, answered letters, and rubber-stamped bills. Occasionally, she lavished pleasure on him, but would always return to her desk quickly.

"Your transgression, slave?" Jana asked in a raised voice.

The slave cleared his throat and answered to the wood paneling in front of his face, unable to turn his head far enough. "I ruined the bed covers of two guest rooms in the west wing when I washed them with the janitors' clothes."

Janice nodded. "You should have smelled it, my dear. Who washes white sheets along with the janitors' clothes? Oil stains all over the good linen."

He bowed his head. "I beg your pardon, Lady Janice. Please punish me."

Jana nodded sternly. This was actual, economic damage the slave had caused.

"I know what you want, and I can put your mind at ease," Janice said, rising. "This place will as tame as a Saturday morning cartoon program tomorrow, my dear.

Don't worry." She raised her eyebrows and grabbed Jana by the wrist. "Because the latest delivery is arriving as we speak. Wanna come and see?"

Jana let Janice drag her through her own first floor. The forty-something's enthusiasm rubbed off on her. They passed through elegant hallways with mirrors and paintings, sumptuous parlors full of antique furniture, and dozens of bedrooms and playrooms. Jana was proud of her work, of her house. Nowhere did the profane specter of sexual use creep through the rooms; here, no chains hung from the walls, no obscure leather contraptions blocked the path, no telltale piles of towels lay beside the beds. Many of the furnishings and furniture were simply what they were meant to be. Their purpose was only apparent to the trained eye of an experienced user. Every lamp sticking out of the wall was reinforced to tie someone to it, every piece of furniture had one too many cushions or backrests, as if they were made for a second person to sit at the feet of the first. The cords and tassels of the bulky curtains could be untied and used as ropes or whips. The beds flaunted majestic canopies, their pillars anchored in the floor, pillars that no slave, however panicked, could tear his chain from them. Janice led Jana to heaven.

The circular room that adjoined the grand entrance hall was lined with soft cushions and was designed to subtly mislead the viewer. An extraordinarily realistic fresco on the ceiling simulated a roof open to the sky, slyly placed columns gave the impression that countless corridors led into the room, yet only formed further niches filled with soft couches and armchairs. "Filled with cushions" was an accurate description: the room had a floor that was best summed up as a circular mattress nine meters in diameter. Janice and Jana paused at its edge, where the marble floor merged into the mattress. A housekeeper waited on the other side of the room in the same position. A large, black leather suitcase stood upright beside her. It reminded one of a coffin. Jana liked this thought. *You will be reborn in my heaven, whoever you may be.* Janice nodded and the housemaid, who was not a slave but a candidate for a position as another mistress in Jana's house, opened the suitcase clasps. Someone audibly startled and a man fell from inside it onto the mattress, into the heavens. The housemaid silently moved away.

The tender little bundle of man looked around, confused and afraid. He was naked, semi-long hair covering his forehead in a modern interpretation of a Beatles hairstyle. Breathing heavily, he soon spotted the richly decorated ceiling where fantastically drawn clouds hung.

Janice clasped her hands together and put them to her chest. "Cute."

Jana nodded.

The young man was eighteen years old at the very most, his body still that of a teenager. He was slender, almost thin. A small pimple sprouted on his neck. He had scratched it. Silly. Jana and Janice got rid of their shoes and stepped onto the mattress barefoot, ready to play.

"Where's Lady Elaine?" he asked in the croaky voice of youth. Janice crouched; Jana did the same. The slave looked anxiously at the two attractive ladies. He was trembling.

Janice pursed her lips. "Lady Elaine told us you want to learn how to be a good boy?"

He nodded sharply. "…yes? But where is she?"

Jana almost sighed in sympathy and brushed his hair aside. He gulped.

Janice placed her warm hand on his thin chest. "Lady Elaine will come pick you up in a while, honey. Do you know where you are?"

He nodded cautiously. "The house."

Jana bowed her head affectionately. "You're with us because Lady Elaine wishes only the best for you." He did not stir, but the trace of a proud smile flitted across his face. "And she told us all about you." The smile disappeared and the two women exchanged a glance.

"You're signed up for six months, honey bunny. So much time to bring out the best in you."

He cleared his throat. "I… I've been accepted?"

Jana nodded. "You're very important to her."

He stuck his chest out and settled into a less exposed position.

Jana almost perished at the sight of him, his innocence and sweetness. "What's your name, sweetheart?" she asked, playfully stroking his belly, which made him jerk back with a giggle.

"Michael," he said.

Janice embraced him and gave him a kiss on his flaming red cheeks. "It seems like you're a good boy already, Michael," she breathed into his ear.

He smiled nervously. "Thank you, Mistress."

The two women's lips formed an astonished O, and they looked at each other. "Such a good boy that you're using correct titles already?"

He nodded shyly, but proudly. Jana put a hand on his chest and sensed a frantically pounding heart. Janice cheekily bit his ear, to which he responded with a sharp gasp.

"Well trained," Jana said, looking deep into his eyes, her lids lowered lasciviously.

"…the face of an angel," Janice continued, the tip of her tongue playing with his lips for a second.

"Slender and healthy," Jana finished, placing her hand on his knee.

Michael quivered at the compliments.

"Wonder why you're here then, wabbit," Janice purred, her hand sliding up his thigh.

Jana pursed her lips in feigned cluelessness and let her hand slide up toward his crotch as well. "Have we been lonely before we met Lady Elaine?"

He nodded.

The women grinned. "Do we have," Janice gripped his arms, "more muscle on one side than the other, little wabbit?"

He fell silent, embarrassed.

Jana's eyes snapped open. "Michael! Did you ruin your pretty head with those women from the Internet?"

He was about to say something, but Janice closed his trembling lips with one finger. "He sure did, Jana. Look at him. No erection."

Jana drew a sharp breath. "No erection?"

Janice shook her head in dismay and pointed between Michael's legs. At this embarrassment, he instinctively pulled his thighs together. Jana thrust her arms to her hips. "Well, where did your manners go all of a sudden, young man?"

He looked back and forth between the two ladies and did not say anything for some time. Jana shook her head in displeasure, "I think we need to cut the excess of self-tenderness out of you, Michael." He kept silent.

Janice seconded her. "I'd say. Arms tied behind his back and a blindfold outside of meal times for two weeks, followed by spankings, good old true school. Plus, if he's one of those cheeky little mattress humpers, an additional restraint during bedtime."

He shook his head. "Mistresses, no, I…"

They laughed. "Ah, so a penis cage is enough to get you out of the habit?"

He nodded at this option. "Yes, Mistresses. A penis cage, please."

Peter liked to state he was in charge of preparing Asian cuisine at home. By that, he actually meant that he was good at cooking up leftover vegetables and meat with rice and soy sauce in a way that tasted surprisingly good. Luisa was a better cook, but even her food was a prize that had to be earned. He set the plates on the table and wished her bon appétit. She reciprocated and quickly reached for her fork.

"Tastes good," she smiled mercifully. He was delighted.

"We had a call with Dodson," he explained, and she looked up at the ceiling for a moment, pondering. "The metal company where the keyword analysis turned out so poorly," he said to help her remember.

"Ah, yes," she lied.

He continued, "The point was that he's not selling products, he's selling his labor. His customers order seventy thousand steel frames in this or that size with very specific dimensions, supply him with the metal, and he actually sells his expertise and the service of making them according to the customer's specifications."

She was already elsewhere in her mind, but he was proud of his profession and continued to speak. "It's a service in a way, but it's also somehow not, because he's not performing the service on the client. Cathrine just goes: 'Niche business, off to SEA with it,' but I had an idea. He's technically acting like a—"

Luisa raised her head and interrupted, "Is Cathrine still wearing those ugly horn-rimmed glasses?"

Trembling little Michael stood naked in the middle of the large dressing room. Surrounded by rolling theater wardrobes and tall closets, he gazed at the walls, only to meet his own eyes, reflected back at him by endless mirrors. Jana loved this sight. She had led countless slaves into this room and every single one – female, male, or anything in between – had taken advantage of the opportunity to sneak a peek at their own butts. Michael was particularly fascinated by his. Admittedly, the two little cheeks were perky, considering the rest of his youthfully scrawny body. Jana certainly appreciated the sight of a tight male bottom and congratulated the unknown Lady Elaine on this catch.

A servant came waving a pink plastic object from an adjoining room. "Yay," she yodeled sweetly and knelt in front of Jana. "This one will fit, Mistress. I'm sure."

Jana accepted the small penis cage. "Thank you, Peaches." Peaches looked up at her owner with big blue eyes. Jana sighed. "Only because you were so quick, darling." She ruffled her knee-length dress. Peaches vanished beneath the skirt hem for an affectionate, intimate kiss.

Carlotta, who happened to be in the dressing room picking out a humiliating tutu for the most muscular, best endowed slave in her collection, slapped Peaches on the bottom. The maid giggled under Jana's skirt. "Thank you, Mistress."

Peter returned from the shower to discover Luisa, stretched out on the couch, watching a series on her tablet. He was wearing a towel tied around his waist. His wet hair fell onto his forehead. He walked around the couch and sat at the end where her feet lay. She sighed knowingly and freed her feet from the warm, cuddly blanket.

Jana walked toward Michael in clicking heels. He stared at the bright pink object. She undid the small clasp and peered into his crotch. "Spread your legs."

He obeyed slowly. Jana smiled patiently. His penis was small, the little sack underneath, it seemed to her, was struggling to grow adequate hair. The entire little male was a snack and looked delicious to devour. He had shaved to please. "Michael," she whispered, stroking his hair, "When this little lock here opens up again, you'll be a different man." She kissed him. He returned the caress immediately, and she almost interrupted the kiss with laughter at his eagerness. He kissed exuberantly, like a movie hero, and also imitated the pompous, rotating, silly neck movement. As his sensory experience focused in on his lips, a lock clicked in his crotch. Jana eased off him and grabbed his arms. "Darling, from now on, we kneel when ladies are present. Understood?"

Luisa's feet rested in Peter's lap. Her toes wrapped around his shaft, and he sighed softly. She hadn't put the tablet away but rather kept watching as she pleasured him with her feet. He was savoring it. He held her socks in front of his nose and inhaled her scent deeply. Feet were by far less suitable for this stimulation than hands. The touch hurt, but he was willing to buy this particular orgasm. She was familiar with his preferences and routinely led him toward climax. Sometimes she would let go of him to make him moan before starting again with a snicker. *Sometimes she enjoys it too*, he assured himself.

"Towel," she demanded absently. "You're moaning already. You're almost there."

He gasped, "M-may I…?" She puffed in annoyance and raised one foot in front of his face, while continuing to massage his glans with the big toe and second toe of her other foot. He stuck out his tongue and slid it into the spaces between her toes. She placed her foot more or less gently on his face, anticipating him on the verge of climax.

Carlotta pushed petite Michael against the white wall.

With only her finger on his chest, she had made him walk backward until he bumped against the white wooden panel with all the gold, mirrored inlays. "On the floor," she said.

He went to his knees. She brushed his face and pushed it back with gentle force until the back of his head throbbed gingerly against the wall. She turned so he could stare directly at her small, round buttocks. She gyrated her hips and pushed her bare ass into his face. She did not actually expect him to try to satisfy her in any way.

With one arm on one of the rolling wardrobes, Jana patiently watched this spiel. This was entirely about learning where one's place was. Michael's face dug deep between Carlotta's ass cheeks, and she nestled deeper against him as she looked over her shoulder severely. This was turf marking, dominance in the flesh. "Don't forget to breathe," she said coldly, and the pulsing of her hips forced his neck into corresponding movements. Someday, he would leave this house. Someday, he would make his Lady Elaine happy. But his nose would forever have been up little Carlotta's ass, up to its root, while his below average cock wriggled in a bright pink penis cage.

Peter came and hurried to hold the bath towel in front of his cock while still climaxing. Luisa pulled her feet back and continued watching her show. He gasped softly and looked at her. "Thank you," he breathed.

She nodded impatiently while the main characters of the soap opera on her tablet accused each other of elaborate intrigues.

CHAPTER 2: THE UNFINISHED

It was nothing special for Peter to attend a meeting with a potential new customer himself. Normally, this task fell to Christian, the charismatic deputy agency manager. As Christian's official substitute, Peter enjoyed the little excursion. Honestly, there were exactly two colleagues at Web Specialists who could hold a candle to him. One of them worked in IT support and made more money with the financial apps he developed on the side than at the agency. The other was Christian. Peter lacked the charisma and cocky business attitude needed for acquisition, but he considered himself an acceptable, competent conversationalist. Christian knew the language of business off the top of his head and could make a "no" sound like a commitment. Peter did not envy him this ability, for he thought it wrong. It was a symptom of a scary business world in which the sheer fear of HR consequences forced people to affirm everything, to say "yes" all the time, to be available. Peter was no anti-capitalist – far from it – but he was intelligent enough to recognize and abhor the strange by-products of a ruthless business world.

The voice from his smartphone told him to turn onto Wilshire Boulevard, and he realized that it had directed him out of the city center and into a suburb. He read the street signs, and although he demonstratively resisted being able to orient himself in this grey city, he recognized some of the names: Clarke-Ring, Veenhouse Alley, Ninneman Road. The prosperous, dusty north of the city. He dimly recalled a conversation with Luisa and her friends about a man from this area whom one of them was lusting after. No significant detail must have dropped, because if it had, he would have remembered the conversation better. His car crested a small hilltop. The houses to the left and right were well kept and marked the visual transition from feudal single-family home to mansion. As a tenant, he could have afforded one of them if Luisa had had a similarly well-paying job, he surmised while turning left as the light turned green.

"You will arrive at your destination in two miles," his smartphone announced.

He raised his eyebrows. "That's almost in the woods," he mumbled to his car's dashboard.

"Well, fuck me," he remarked to that same dashboard two kilometers later. He had reached his destination. "I didn't know Count Dracula needed a website." He drove through a gated stone archway toward a huge mansion that might as well call itself a castle with impunity. Gravel crunched beneath the tires of his station wagon. Cultivated meadows lined the gently curving driveway. A giant weeping willow dipped its branches into an almost black pond. A woman in coveralls stood in its midst, clearing it of duckweed by means of what looked like a giant, netted spoon. The sun was shining on a small park area that included the lake and the weeping willow. The other houses in the area were two hundred yards down the road. Anyone who wanted to reach the archway had to take one last steep turn and head straight for it.

He stopped in a large courtyard in front of the massive, wooden front door. A stone staircase rose in five steps toward the portal. The only thing missing, Peter contemplated in a mixture of excitement and a little irony, were two grotesque lion statues with their paws on weathered globes, and the luxurious private home of a James Bond villain would have been complete. A sculpture above the grand portal exuded diabolical flair: the beautiful, yet distorted with rage, face of a Medusa gazed down on the courtyard, thc serpents around her head craning their necks, ready to lunge forward. Peter got out of his car and shouldered the carrying case for his laptop. When he pressed the button on the key, the blinkers lit up, and the portal opened.

A good-looking woman in a pastel, knee-length dress appeared on the steps. Her dark blonde hair ought to have seemed ordinary, but lovely waves in it promised the unbridled joie de vivre of a wild mop of curls without robbing its owner of the grace of straight hair. She smiled from a beautiful face with bright brown eyes to which the sunlight gave the glow of wild honey. Peter prided himself on his vocabulary, and the best description for this woman seemed to be "otherworldly." The spectacular blonde cast challenging waves that played the eye, and she shared the light brown of her eyes with innumerable people, but they had a depth that made prolonged eye contact a risk.

"I've gotta say," Peter explained, surprised at his own bravado, "This house would fit an older gentleman with a white cat in his lap, dramatically turning in his office chair. 'Welcome to my secret base, Special Agent.'"

Jana put her head back and laughed out loud. Her bell-bright voice made Peter smile involuntarily. "Maybe I'm just the supervillain's charming secretary, Mr. Wartmann."

He shook his head. "I'll eat my hat if you're anyone's secretary, Mrs.…?"

She tilted her head gently, the waves of her hair seconding the almost imperceptible movement. Peter's gaze subconsciously slid up to the Medusa above her. "Ms. Jana," she said, and they shook hands.

I may as well have introduced myself by Winnie the Pooh, Peter thought and snorted audibly.

His hostess sassily raised her eyebrows. "Don't worry. I have a last name, which you'll find out, of course… if we get down to business."

He nodded with a smile, enjoying the amusing exchange. "Why did I imagine the head of the mysterious ladies of the house to be exactly like that?"

She smiled broadly. "Because you are a smart man, Mr. Wartmann. Please," she said, pointing to the portal, "I have coffee made."

"We're going to make this a very special game, handsome," Selina whispered, biting the tip of Michael's nose. He didn't flinch, but a pained hiss betrayed his torment. The young man had been assigned to Selina for the day, and in her capacity as the cultural tutor of the house, she wanted to make him a special welcome gift.

Due to Jana's important appointment, which could take up the large office as well as several of the main rooms and, at unpredictable times, the hallways, her play options were limited. Space wasn't the only thing constrained though. Nudity was forbidden in the hallways today, and no loud games or overly revealing screams were allowed to take place or be heard. Selina, though, was a resourceful woman. Her raven curls vibrated in anticipation. Michael stood in the middle of her reading room. The large study table with its bendable lights had been pushed aside to make room for a slim, wooden frame. Selina had discovered this toy just recently; not even she had known of the existence of this apparatus.

As she gazed at the simple frame made of a three-legged base weighted with marble, a single pole rising waist high, and a finely ornamented bracket at its top, Michael sighed hard. Like every item in Jana's house, this one was an object with two sides to it. If Selina had shown it to a musician, they would have guessed it an antique music stand with additional weight at its lowest point. Perhaps it was meant for cellists to lean their heavy instrument against it? The slender metal clamps, with which the thin pages of a music book could supposedly be held at the top, were extraordinarily well suited for threading and fixing a penis through them. Given it was a small penis.

"Through there," she said softly, tapping the rack with a baton.

Michael looked at her, aghast. "M-my penis through the o-opening?"

Selina's gaze was icy. "Michael, I've seen a lot of penises in my life and that thing between your legs doesn't really deserve that label. So, your weenie, including the cage, through here, please." She uttered the request with such venomous politeness that he shivered instinctively and complied with her instruction.

He approached the music stand and unbent the two metal holders. Selina slowly nodded. He slid his member, including the humiliating chastity device, through the gap he had created and closed the holder again. Selina locked the unorthodox frame in place with a flick of the two small mechanical levers under the board that was supposed to hold the spine of a music book.

Michael now stood in the middle of the room, genitalia attached to a waist-high, unusually heavy, music stand.

Jana led her guest into the entrance hall. Mr. Wartmann was a bright, sharp-witted man who had surprised her with casual banter. She remembered her guess and was glad not to be welcoming an aging analyst in a corduroy suit or a youngster with a PC into her domicile. All right, Mr. Wartmann was not a beauty, but a man in his mid-thirties who was obviously confident in his abilities and who could easily give his office body more shape by exercising twice a week. She had liked his wit.

She spread her arms in the massive, ebony-and-marble flaunting entrance hall. "I welcome you, thus officially, to my house, Mr. Wartmann."

He puffed out his cheeks. "I am impressed, Ms. Jana. Do you have royal ancestry?"

Yes, she said to herself, *but that's none of your business yet, Mister Search Engine Optimizer*. "I'm the lucky owner. Let's leave it at that for now."

He grinned lopsidedly, and Jana knew he was thinking the right thing. He nodded professionally. "As I said, I'm absolutely impressed. You mentioned coffee?"

Selina sat down as she positioned her chair in front of the music stand. She was wearing an all-white, widely unbuttoned blouse, a red pencil skirt, and a pair of stunning, pointy-toed high heels. Black nylon tights clung around her legs. She sat in front of the standing-straight Michael and slipped off both shoes.

He watched her with looks that would have earned him a slap in the face.

Her slender fingers placed the high heels accurately beside the armchair, and she crossed her legs. A tense silence fell. She spread her tiny toes, freed from the confines of the footwear. Where her skin stretched the black fabric widest, it became nearly transparent. A hint of her pedicure loomed. She tilted her head with a smile. "Do you like feet, Michael?"

A blissful shiver ran down her spine. It was so unusual and, done right, irritating to address people by their first names, clearly and frequently, in personal conversation. For a young man like him, who was certainly called "Mick" or "Mike" all the time, something as banal as the mere mention of one's own name had to be an especially stirring experience. Probably, Selina thought, watching his trembling mouth open for a response, only his mother called him by his full name.

"I-I think your feet are w-wonderful, Mistress Selina," he stammered. She sighed and raised her leg. The way the obscure contraption showcased his caged cock and ball sack, she could comfortably press the sole of her foot against it, her heel on the wood, the plastic of the cage under her toes, millimeters from his reddened, craving skin. His testicles were level with the foremost part of her sole, the slightest application of force would squeeze them between her foot and the metal behind, causing severe pain.

"Michael," she repeated, certain her words were literally boring into his mind, "You haven't really seen my feet yet. Besides, I asked if you liked feet, not if you liked *my* feet."

He inhaled sharply, his cheeks reddening. "I beg forgiveness, Mistress Selina. I like feet a lot, yes."

She nodded understandingly and very definitively, as if the silliest student of a very patient teacher had finally understood a certain lesson. "Terrific. You'll love our game then. It's quite simple," she explained, clearing her throat. "I will ask questions, you will answer. If you answer all questions correctly, you get to take the pantyhose I'm wearing to your room and spend the night without a cage." She pursed her lips. "Something I would imagine that would make you very happy, wouldn't it?" She turned her foot a little on his privates, and he groaned in pain.

"Y-yes, Mistress Selina."

She nodded. "That's the grand prize. If you answer even a single question wrong, though, it's forfeit."

He nodded.

"Wrongly answered questions lead to ouchies," she purred, pushing against his cock with more force for half a second, causing a sickening twinge in his abdomen and a helpless whimper. "There's a special rule, though: we can't be noisy, Michael. Lady Jana has an important appointment and does not wish for her little toys to make themselves known. Do we understand?" She increased the pressure, and he broke off his own shriek, mustering all the strength he had.

"Aaow-hrrrrnnngh!"

Selina grinned. "Well done."

Ms. Jana's office was as wonderfully surreal as its owner, Peter thought. She opened a door of whitewashed wood, and he stepped into a kind of Victorian studio that had been stylishly transplanted into the 21st century. Two flat-screen monitors protruded from an elegant desk, and somehow the overall design of the room managed to keep the sober electronics from breaking with the aging starkness of the furnishings. Two leather-covered sitting shells sat in front of the desk, and a chandelier hung from the ceiling.

"Why," he wondered, looking at his hostess, "Is this place not world famous yet?"

She nodded. "You're hanging in the wrong social circles, Mr. Wartmann. We are world famous. In a sense."

He returned the confident smile. "Enlighten me. In our pursuit, knowledge is literally money and the foundation of success."

She pointed to the two sitting shells. "With pleasure."

Jana could have slapped her across the face when Carlotta entered the room, grinning broadly and carrying in a pot of coffee and two mugs. The young mistress wore a modest costume that seemed appropriate for a personal assistant and poured them coffee, cheekily leaning over his shoulder, offering an intimate view down her blouse. Peter Wartmann did not look down her cleavage but thanked the unknown woman politely. *Not bad, Mr. Wartmann.* When they had both taken a sip, Jana took a deep breath. Carlotta disappeared with a fat grin. Cheeky minx.

"I have to apologize preemptively," Jana said. "My knowledge of your subject is so limited that it embarrasses me, especially as a CEO with the responsibility of running a company for profit."

Peter Wartmann put aside his nonchalance, and his expression changed. Jana looked into two eyes that seemed to shift from the color of a lively, yet not particularly rapid, mountain stream to that of a deep ocean. They had entered his domain, and he was well armed. *How exciting.*

Instinctively, she leaned forward as he opened his mouth.

"Do you think advertising is money thrown out the window?" he asked.

She shook her head. "No."

He took a sip of coffee. "With that, you know more about my trade than half of my other clients."

Jana laughed out loud. "Nemesis," a curse only used in the house slipped out. "You must have terrible clients."

He shook his head, even though the odd word had thrown him off for a moment. "To agree would be unprofessional."

She grinned. "But true."

He remained ironclad, earning even more of her respect. "I'm sure we can put a great website together."

Jana refilled her coffee. "I'm already convinced of that," she said with a smirk.

Mr. Wartmann leaned back. "The first and most important question: why is there not even a *bad* website so far? Why is there literally nothing about your house on the Internet?"

Jana thought for a moment. "There was a website. Years ago. It had too much success with the wrong demographic." Peter Wartmann nodded slowly. She didn't blame him; how could he understand what the ladies took to be the wrong target audience?

"Meaning?" was his curt follow-up question.

"Meaning… I should explain to you how the house works."

"What are the first three notes of the solmized C major scale?" asked Selina, eyeing Michael's face with the confident, friendly interest of a dedicated teacher. Bewilderment and the certainty that he would not be allowed to go to bed tonight with his willy free and her worn nylon pantyhose settled on him. Selina leaned forward as there was still no response after ten seconds, only a shocked breath out. She chanted softly, "Do-Re-

Miiiii…" At the third step, she pressed her foot against his wedged sack. He hissed painfully, bit his lip, and threw his upper body violently back in panic. The heavy base of the music stand prevented escape. She shook her head, eyes wide. "There goes the grand prize, Michael." He whimpered through clenched teeth and actually managed not to scream. "Go on, darling," she declared, taking her foot back and clearing her throat. "How many stanzas are there in Franz Schubert's 'Unfinished'?"

"Basically, we are an accommodations-and-lodging business and have more in common with a hotel or a spa than any dominatrix parlor or red-light establishment," Jana said. "There are women, wealthy women, who have a very hard time finding men who meet their standards. By that, I don't mean rich ladies who worry about the sincerity of their pool-boy disguised lover."

He nodded.

"I'm talking about women who live a dominant lifestyle and don't want to turn to the usual dating websites or clubs, or *cannot* because of their position, which, although there are good places, I can understand. We are a training facility for men who hope to appeal to one of these women and eventually – caution: 'bad' word ahead – want to be *bought* by a woman."

Peter's eyes widened. His mind buzzed with visions of jet set women, walking men on leashes across red carpets. He must've unknowingly shaken his head in disbelief, as Jana insisted: "We're talking matchmaking here. We train the perfect partners for dominant ladies. This is our main source of income. Everything is voluntary, mind you – every man has the right to pack his bags and leave if he so chooses. However, we're facing an extremely difficult problem: the type of man we *want* to appeal to doesn't hang around on the usual BDSM dating portals, messaging women and asking if he can buy their shoes or if they'd like to whip his butt. The type of man who can be formed profitably by us has an excellent educational background and is intelligent and unfulfilled at the same time. He maintains dead relationships, crashes into invisible walls in his everyday life, walls that seem to exist only for him. Most of the men who find us are what we call 'late bloomers.' Young men, pushing 30, who end up with a therapist or a dominatrix, full of frustration after their latest failed relationship. Both women pursue the same profession, by the way."

The conviction with which she said this stifled the surprised laughter in Peter's throat.

"In most cases" – now she smirked, and he realized she felt great affection for the men she accommodated in her house – "they're men who don't really relate to their own success. It is the loveliest of *non-failed livelihoods* we gather here. Unfortunately, this type of man is very rare." She sighed. "In addition, they often don't even know what their problem is. Those who visit a dominatrix because of a small predisposition like a sexual fetish can be found and referred here. The practicing ladies outside the house know us and know when a man is a candidate for us. They receive a small profit share on the sale. The therapists we work with are more cautious and recommend us only in rare cases. We owe our status as an urban legend to the not always ideal recommendations of medical therapists. You said you researched us?"

"Wrong," Selina said, squeezing. Michael screamed with his mouth closed. An enervating, shrill chirp sounded as he did so. She listened calmly. The baton spun on her palm as her foot pressed against Michael's privates, trapping his testicles between her sole and the wooden pole. Selina had plenty of time. Michael's torso tossed about. His thin little fists pounded against the wood. His mouth threatened to open and let the scream burst. She sighed and took her foot off his penis. "This isn't gonna work, Michael. I was assured you were a smart boy." '

He groaned in relief, his weary torso tilting toward her. His half-long hair fell into his eyes, and he wailed softly. Selina pitifully clicked her tongue and lifted her foot under his forward-bent face. “Poor wabbit. Here, do a little sniffy-sniff.” She wiggled her toes beneath Michael’s nose, and he took a deep breath.

She smiled softly. “Good boy.”

He began to move his lips as the stabbing pain in his abdomen subsided.

“Not with your mouth,” she clarified, and he ceased the movement of his lips in order to lower his nose. She spread her toes and let the tip of his nose dip into the elastic fabric, “I’m being so good to you,” she explained as she did so.

He nodded imperceptibly. “Thank you, Mistress Selina.”

She played with the baton between her fingers. “Will you be a good boy and answer my questions correctly from now on?”

“I have done some research, yes. There are threads on closed forums, a comment here and there, a question with no proper answers on an abandoned dating site. Many believe you are a marketing stunt by the dominatrixes in town.”

Jana laughed. “Ah, the ruthless Lady Regina Sadistica Maxima and the even more merciless Mistress Bernadette of Painville, yes. These two ladies have nothing to do with us. They know us, but they maintain a very traditional view of their craft.” Peter wrinkled his brow. Jana winked. “Classic dominance. An hour of flogging costs a $150, with a gas mask and fixation on the pillory another $50. If you want to see more skin than an exposed kneecap between my pitch-black leather dress and riding boots, we start talking $200, laddie.” Smiling broadly, she indicated a whipping motion with her hand. “Whik-tch!”

Peter laughed. “I see. Do you disapprove?”

Jana shook her head. "No. They are where we came from. The raw, studded-and-spiked origins, resisting an inflexible society. A little too dark, a little too repellent, a little too much 'biker,' yet necessary for the time. I'm sure every client of those two ladies I mentioned is extremely satisfied and happy."

He believed to understand and cleared his throat. "Anyway, there is little more than speculation about your house and you, Ms. Jana. I think that's a good starting position."

She took a sip of coffee and frowned into the steam rising from the cup. "Mmm? Aren't we supposed to be about visibility?"

He opened his bag. "Visibility with the right people, Ms. Jana."

"Felix Mendelssohn Bartholdy's no less talented sister was known as?" Selina asked, holding her baton to her mouth as knowingly as mischievously. Michael's eyes widened at the onset of more pain. He realized he wasn't here to answer questions, but to be played with. Selina nodded with deliberation. Understanding about his situation seeped into his mind. His shoulders slumped, and his mouth vibrated briefly as he considered guessing some name and quickly dismissed the fatal idea. His eyes cleared. His mind steeled itself to resist the unpleasant sensory stimulus that would surely set in immediately if he shook his head. Selina relished this moment. Her foot lifted from his cock and drove to his lips. "No answer, Michael?" He kept his lips tightly closed, not opening them to suck greedily on her toes. He even held his breath to keep from inhaling her scent. She bit her lip. "You're learning."

"How many, erm…" Peter gestured searchingly with one hand while his laptop loaded.

Jana tilted her head with a lovely flick of her eyes. "Yes?" She perfectly understood but was paying him back good naturedly for the cheeky little banter he had traded with her earlier.

"How many *slaves* do you sell – roughly – a month?" The unusual words slipped his lips with difficulty.

Jana's mouth opened to a broad smile. Her brown eyes developed the pull Peter had felt when he'd met her. "Zero." He punched in his password and hummed, "Ohh… 'kay?"

Jana sighed. "We stay afloat with short training classes. Women bring their slaves in for certain courses or rent a part of the building for a period of time. Like I said, we're a lodging business. Our main source of income, which I described to you, is not quantity. For that reason, we are turning to you." He raised his head while several SEO and keyword programs booted up, making the fan on his laptop whisper hoarsely. "You should ask," Jana explained, leaning forward, "how many we've sold in our twenty-four years." He just nodded. "Thirteen," she smiled.

Peter's jaw dropped, and he reached for his coffee mug. "Kudos. Then the individual chaps must have cost quite a bit if" – he gestured to the surrounding area – "all this is profitable despite the low sales figures, sustained by rental income and slaves on short-term training." He could have laughed at his new vocabulary, but he took the formidable woman across him too seriously to do so.

She waited to answer until the cup touched his lips. "I guess you could say so. A young, well-trained slave from our house costs between two hundred and six hundred thousand."

He almost choked on his coffee.

Michael clung to the metal frame of the music rack and gasped, whimpered, and quivered. Selina's foot squeezed mercilessly. He started to wail, so she twisted her foot and played with the testicles beneath her sole. The resulting pain went a wee bit too far, so the scream finally burst from his throat, loud and unrelenting, filling the salon with the thin boy's hidden strength. She eased away from him and smiled.

"Did you hear that?" Peter asked.

Jana rolled her eyes. "I had asked for silence very insistently, but it seems that my staff are poor at receiving of orders." He chugged down his coffee somberly, and Jana almost giggled. "Excuse me, Mr. Wartmann, but your expression is just magnificent. I assure you – nothing happens here to guest or staff that is not part of the play and agreed upon." He nodded silently and put down his cup. Jana leaned back and crossed her legs. "I know that there's something like an architecture to a website." She was ashamed of his unease at the shout and directed him back to the world of analysis and optimization in which he carried himself so confidently.

He coughed. "Right. Starting from a home page, we can work on various topics and present them in an optimized way. So, speaking freely and without much prior knowledge, we could set up a section for the short-term offers, explaining the individual courses. Then a section for the ladies who rent parts of the building for a weekend. And, of course, a page that appeals to the rare type of man you create your most important product from."

Jana nodded, tapping her foot. So far, Peter had held it together with bravado, not staring at her feet. He would remain steadfast. She noticed how hard he was straining to maintain eye contact. "I want a single page," she said slowly, yet with determination. "A single page for the men we wish to find us."

Peter smiled softly, trying hard not to come off with the arrogance of a professional. "Ms. Jana, a website thrives on the traffic that takes place on it. We need pages with links to each other, context for the algorithm to read and interpret."

She understood but had already made a decision. "A single page, optimized."

He sighed. "I can create a single page for you but can't promise success. If we put all your skills and accomplishments on one huge, bloated page, the information we're trying to convey will be so large and vague that the search engine will think it's poorly done and rank it accordingly."

Jana reflected for a moment. "I don't have a huge page full of enticing offers, picture galleries, and customer reviews in mind" – she smirked at this notion – "but a succinct explanation of what's going on and a big button for applying here."

Peter understood and typed around indecisively in his keyword tool. "You want an SEO-optimized sign-up page. I've done something similar for a newspaper before."

She nodded quietly and fixated on him. "So it's possible?"

He shrugged. "Yes, it is possible, but the results could be bad or wholly absent – which would be equally bad."

"Wouldn't it be possible to put all the important things on the page, but… not discernable? So that they are there, but don't get noticed by visitors?" Jana scrunched up her face apologetically at her lack of knowledge and the potentially stupid question.

He smiled at her. "That's how it worked way back. So-called 'meta' keywords. There are many little tricks we can use, but the search engine punishes this once we're caught. Transparency and sincerity will rank us high. Good content that is relevant to the target group and presented in an appealing way is the golden rule. Expertise, trust and authoritativeness."

Jana laughed abruptly. "Why does this sound like it's taken straight from some 'How to be a dominatrix' guide?" Peter joined in her laughter. She glared at him for a few seconds, then sighed. "I'm serious about the single page, Mr. Wartman. You must understand that we are treading a paradoxical path: We don't want to be found. Unless the seeker is an absolute bull's-eye."

He understood her very well and his professionalism dictated only one response. "Then I can't guarantee you success and can only promise a visually appealing site."

She nodded. "I'd rather no one finds it at all than a single one of the type we're not looking for."

"…but Esmeralda grabbed his strong hand. 'I won't let you go without one last kiss, Pablo,' she said, and her gaze glowed hot as Andalusian fire. Pablo, already facing his black Cat—, er, Cadillac in the parking lot, stood in the doorway, not turning to her. With the coldness of bitter disappointment, he said—"

Selina cleared her throat. Michael looked up from the trashy little novel. "Yes, Mistress Selina?"

She moaned listlessly and applied more pressure on his nutsack. He jerked fearfully. "Sweet Michael," she purred, "The characters are hot-blooded Spaniards and we're here to practice reading. Your Mistress expects you to return a charming, cultured little slave. *Please*," she emphasized the unusual word, "I don't want to give you any more boo-boos, my little wabbit. A little more enthusiasm when reading aloud."

CHAPTER 3: DORMANT SHAPES

"Believe it or not," Jana said, closing the door, "This is the first time I'm giving a tour of the facility."

Peter tilted his head and merely produced a platitude. "There's a first time for everything, I guess."

She nodded. "Absolutely. I gave instructions – in vain, as we heard – to keep a low profile. We still shouldn't encounter any naked people in the corridors, and there will be no overly extravagant measures today."

He snorted and followed her down a jade carpeted hallway. "Measures? Is that what you call the S&M practices here?"

Jana turned and let him lead the way up a large white marble staircase. "Simply put, yes. However, very little of what we do revolves around pure pleasure. Sure, we rent our premises to approved couples who use them for that purpose, but every measure has a meaning."

He nodded. "Tuition, just in a very special way."

Jana opened her hands. "Exactly." She directed him to the heavens at the foot of the stairs. Peter marveled at the glistening, bright room with its elaborate fresco and the gigantic expanse of upholstery in its center. Jana observed his wandering gaze. Did he grasp the intent of the apparently haphazardly scattered furniture? At least, it seemed to her, his understanding of her problem had deepened.

"You've told me about the kind of man you consider worthy of being trained as your primary product," he continued after she had led him out of the heavens and into one of the many bedrooms. A globe the size of a desk stood in the corner, tall windows casting sharp rays of bright sunlight into the room. He carefully touched the globe and trailed his fingers over the ancient, flawed representation of Earth. She folded her arms behind her back and didn't make the mistake of interrupting him. "It's going to be incredibly difficult to put up a site that will be found by the very men who are otherwise referred here by dominatrixes or therapists. What are these people looking for? We can hardly write 'training to become a high-class slave for rich women' without appealing to the men you don't want. At the same time, we mustn't get too off-the-wall, or there might be misunderstandings."

Jana's otherworldly non-and-yet-again curls seconded her happy nod. "That's exactly our problem." *Clever fellow, Mr. Wartmann.*

"The most intriguing phobia," Selina explained, her little baton stroking the bridge of Michael's nose, "is also the cutest. Erythrophobia. Ring a bell?" He shook his head. Selina waited a second, then pinched his nose mischievously. "I don't hear anything."

He growled nasally, "No, Mistress Selina, it doesn't."

She let go and rolled her eyes. "The fear of blushing."

His eyes froze; he took a startled breath, and she licked her lips. "How did you…?"

Her stare made him fall abruptly silent. "I'm skilled," she revealed. "It is my special talent to recognize, address, and eradicate the flaws in my protégés." He nodded and cocked his head; she was trying to rid him of a flaw he knew he had. She proudly slapped his bare bottom.

"That's it! That's exactly the reaction I want, Michael." He nodded and his flaming red cheeks only validated his passion. Selina stepped right in front of him. He was still standing in the middle of her reading room, pinned to the music stand. She wrapped her arms around his chest and gently cradled him from left to right without pulling too hard. He timidly raised his arms to return the gesture, and she allowed it. When she lifted her head from his shoulder, his eyes were glassy. She pressed a kiss on his flaming cheeks.

"You're blushing because you're scared, wabbit. I can make the fear go away," she promised in a childlike whisper. "But you'll have to be an obedient boy to do so."

He nodded distinctly. "I am an obedient boy, Mistress Selina."

"In marketing, we call it the 'sales chain,'" Peter said as Jana led him down a flight of stairs, into the basement. "Not to be confused with the supply chain." The sound of running water echoed, and a female voice laughed. "Feature, benefit, use. That's how you sell things." He was thinking out loud rather than speaking. Jana let him, as he was obviously quite taken in by the challenge her problem presented. She had to touch him by the elbow to escort him to the spa of the house; he would have walked straight into the laundry. "We mustn't bring up the problem," he concluded, and a brief, surprisingly fiery glance struck her before he continued muttering, downright ignoring his surroundings. A pity, in a way, Jana thought, looking up at the pompous waterspout that fed a lavish swimming pool. The epic statue of an Amazon with bare feet stood triumphantly over a slain Minotaur, water flowing from its mouth into the pool. The bathing ladies and their slaves wore bikinis and swimming shorts, a fact Jana received with grateful glances. Peter Wartmann halted. She almost walked into him.

"This mosaic is great," he remarked, pointing at a stone

mural.

"It doesn't fit the ancient Greek theme," Jana confessed, "But I am admittedly proud of it."

Peter scratched his temple. "It represents the underworld, doesn't it?"

Jana buzzed reproachfully. "Almost. It's Dante Alighieri's nine circles of hell. A fitting motif for a basement."

Peter laughed out loud. "Absolutely. But gloomier than the rest of the house."

Jana nodded. "Down here, I'll be honest, the more mundane activities take place: bathing and splashing about. Over there stands the victorious, female Amazon and the subjugated, male Minotaur. Here" – she pointed – "the menacing circles of hell. That back there is the splash-proof copy of a painting of Poseidon. Quite appropriate. A swimming pool calls for entertainment, not high culture."

Peter commented, "It's allowed to be a bit more placative here, you mean."

She winked. "Exactly."

"You' re wonderful," she whispered and opened the two metal brackets of the music rack. Michael gently smiled and pulled his privates out of the contraption. The small plastic cage clacked on the wood, and Selina giggled. "If you're good, you'll get to come out eventually," she purred and bent down to stroke the plastic. Michael proudly stretched his back. She stroked his testicles and cradled the two little balls in her palm. "A while longer."

He agreed, nodding intelligently. With an energetic twist, she turned to her chair. "Up there" – she gestured to a shelf – "the poetry book with the roman numeral 'six.'" He crossed the room, reached onto the shelf, returned, and handed her the book. Selina let him put it on the armchair and reached for her skirt. "Take off Mistress' nylon pantyhose, Michael." He went to his knees, a motion she answered with an affirming smile. His slender hands traveled up her legs, standing out clearly as slithering silhouettes beneath the tight skirt. She nodded at him in affirmation, maintaining eye contact. He grasped the nylon seam and slowly pulled it. The black peeled from her snow-white skin with maddening slowness. Michael's gaze followed with fascination, something she adjusted by quickly placing her index finger under his chin. He looked into her eyes. She nodded slowly as the warm fabric continued to run down her legs, emitting a subtle scent, and finally lay at her ankles. She reached for the book, sank into the chair behind her, and stretched a foot. He raised his hands to slip the pantyhose over her heel and fully release her foot. She shook her head. "With your teeth."

"How helpful would it be if I showed you more of the premises?" Jana asked.

Peter was grateful for the resonating offer to bring the tour of the vast house to an end. "I think I would benefit much more from further conversation with you."

Jana smiled. *Your work should benefit, Mr. Wartmann, your work.*

"I have a rough idea of the things we want to say," he explained, "but haven't found the right words yet. I need to create a wireframe, fill it with some scribble, and then we'll have something to work with."

Jana didn't entirely understand what he meant but nodded politely as they reached her office. "I'm at your service."

He produced his smartphone. "Thank you. I'll get back to you later this week," he explained. "For now, I need to let what I've seen sink in a little."

Jana chuckled and winked playfully. "I must have made a great impression."

Peter opened his mouth in shock. "Oh dear! Sorry. What I meant to say was that I now understand what problem we have to solve. I didn't mean to flee from you at all."

Jana's eyes bound his gaze. "Don't worry. I wouldn't have the means to prevent you from escaping, Mr. Wartmann." They both laughed and Jana accompanied him to his car.

"Well?" Cathrine asked.

Peter snorted. "It's… strange."

His coworker crossed her arms. "Not a brothel, is it?"

He snapped his laptop into the docking station on his glass desk. "No, definitely not that. It's a huge facility. Swimming pool, baroque rooms, marble, a room made entirely of upholstery. I can barely describe it."

She bit her tongue and looked around for a moment. "Did you… get to see some action?"

Peter leaned his head back in amusement and sank into his office chair. "No, it was extremely low-key. At one point, someone suddenly screamed loudly" – Cathrine held her hand over her mouth, cackling as he spoke – "But other than that, just a few people taking a dip. They might as well have been splashing around in any random swimming pool. The facility, however, is absolute insanity."

It was late. His colleague Sandra had already left, so Cathrine unceremoniously sat down in her office chair. "All kinds of devices, studs, spikes and chains?"

He laughed at her curiosity. Peter enjoyed talking to her. "As a matter of fact, no. Everything was just so… a level beyond, you know? As if" – he winked – "as if Queen Victoria had set up an S&M studio."

"She's having a house party!" Luisa said with a smile, looking at Peter as if he ought to be able to draw an important, exhilarating conclusion from this information. He did understand that she was talking about her friend Anna's birthday party, but he had failed to come across the important core information that he was apparently supposed to extract. Luisa rolled her eyes. "She'll invite

Robbie!" she said, widening her eyes and mouth into a "how awesome is that?" facial expression.

Peter remembered. "Ah, okay. Is she into him at last?"

Luisa raised her eyebrows in amusement. "When Robbie comes, there's no way she's inviting Jonas. Nobody liked him anyway. So it'll be a little more relaxed for you, too, because there'll be at least two men there. Maybe three, if Jasmin brings her boyfriend, but she doesn't know yet."

Peter took a bite of his corn on the cob. Luisa had cooked and it wasn't dinner, but a brunch laced with vogue spices, which he dutifully praised. "Cool," he said flatly. A wink and a harmless, tongue-in-cheek remark about being "glad not to be alone with you chattering chicks" would have suited the exchange, but Luisa didn't like that sort of thing. She ironically lowered her fork into her plate, "'Cool, yeah.' Thanks, Mister Talkative."

Peter laughed. "Sorry. My mind was on my work. Important wireframe tomorrow, and the client is quite demanding." He could count on her not to follow up.

"Mmh!" she made excitedly, lifting the little skewers jabbed into her corn on the cob before taking a bite. "I had the weirdest guy on the phone today. His name was – no shit – Liu Holzmeyer. An Asian, but with a German last name. You can't imagine how his accent sounded! I asked Corinna if she had ever had any contact with him, and she said he was somewhere in Hong Kong. Anyway, today he was trying to say 'parcel tracking,' but because of his accent, it totally sounded—"

Banal, Peter thought.

"Look closely," Selina ordered, taking a macaron. "Fourteen is so good. You'll learn, I guarantee." Michael nodded and stood beside her, obviously forlorn with his silver tray of sweet baked goods in the large auditorium. Selina sighed with relish. "Whoa, these are nothing to scoff at either." She flicked her finger, whereupon he immediately turned the tray back to her. "Did you bake these, wabbit?"

He smiled proudly, and his narrow back swelled. "Yes, Mistress Selina. Lady Derya has given me permission to use the rest of the dough up." With these words, his croaky, almost youthful voice picked up in strength quite decidedly, and he pointed to a crescent-shaped pastry. "This one has a small amount of anise added to it. Lady Derya has praised it highly."

Selina hummed contentedly. "That smile, Michael, is as sexy as ten six-pack abs. Are you my little culinary superhero?"

He nodded with flaming red cheeks. "Yes, Mistress Selina."

She winked at him. "Aww! I'm melting, wabbit."

A grin was stuck to his face as he watched his pretty Mistress Selina eat his cookies.

The evening promised delicate entertainment for everyone living in the house – from Lady Jana to the youngest, newest slave. Everyone gathered in the auditorium, which took up almost the entire east wing of the house.

Jana sat in a loge and promptly thought that a gilded opera glass and a softly fluttering fan would suit her, but she was not that decadent. The curtain on the stage, which should have been red, was midnight blue. Three black and blue prompter boxes bulged out from the edge of the stage in the oval, yet irregular shape of mussels. Jana smiled thievishly and swayed in her chair. Today's slave, a sweet thing named Lana, whom she called Lilith, reacted to Jana's delight and stretched her head, which until just now had been leaning against her right thigh. Jana put her hands on Lilith's cheeks. "I'm so excited, my lovely," she purred, giving Lilith a kiss. "A fine man who will help us find the right slaves for the auctions visited today."

Lilith nodded happily. "That's great, my Mistress."

Jana bit Lilith's lower lip, humming lustfully. "Rmmwah! Oh, you bet."

Janice entered the loge, and Jana's hands left Lilith's face. Lilith's eyes lit up, and two sweet bite marks appeared on her lip. In the house, ladies didn't ask if they were intruding on an intimate moment. Janice just winked at Lilith and sat down. "Who's playing today, ladies?"

Jana tapped the toe of her shoe against Lilith's bare thigh; the slave immediately started helping her out of her shoes. "Fourteen and Peaches," Jana explained.

Janice rejoiced. "Wow! I'm totally into Peaches."

Jana, allowing Lilith to massage her bare feet, looked down into the lower seats. The auditorium in no way resembled the true dimensions of a real theater building, but the funnel design of seat rows converging on the stage, the loges in the walls, and the soft carpeted walkways were as genuine as in any opera. The audience made the real difference. Jana's house accommodated more than the seventeen ladies she counted among her inner circle of close associates, as well as their small contingent of personal servants. About a hundred people had gathered in the theater, awaiting the start of the performance. Jana enjoyed the view over the inhabitants of her small, secret realm. Some of the ladies seized the theater performances for "real" dates with their male slaves, allowing them to wear tuxedos. Most were allowed to sit next to or beneath their ladies. Naked skin was omnipresent. The scent of lust filled the high-ceilinged room. Selina waved to her from below; Jana returned the salute. Slender Michael held a tray of what might have been pastries. Hard to tell from up here. Selina seemed pleased with him.

The midnight blue curtain slowly opened, and the lights dimmed. Quiet applause erupted. Behind the curtain, a sand-colored room was unveiled, with a bed in the middle. Amphorae and statues featuring the heads of hawks, jackals, and crocodiles lined the walls, and a window revealed the rooftops of a colorful desert metropolis. The beautiful Peaches, a black wig on her head, dressed in countless necklaces, bangles of gold and blue and green gems, lolled in white sheets. Whispered words emanated from cleverly hidden speakers; someone occasionally shouted something in a foreign language, and the metallic song of crossing blades rang out. A large, wooden door flew open. Two men in golden breastplates tumbled into it backwards and remained lying on the stone floor, cut down by an unknown assailant outside the door.

Fourteen was a tall, lean man with a broad chest and short, dark brown curls. He entered the sand-colored room, armed with a bronze sword, and directed a fiery gaze at the sighing Peaches writhing on the bed. Fourteen wore a blue toga that fell in countless folds, and a golden laurel wreath sat on his stern-looking head. His delicately lined face was the Mediterranean equivalent of James Dean, and his abrupt, energetic motions were evidence of incredible power that virtually oozed from his pores.

Peaches laughed throatily and gathered the white, softly crackling sheets. "Too late, Octavian," she said, lifting an arm from the sheets. Two small, red wounds bore witness to the bite of a poisonous snake. "Your intrigues are at last bearing sweet fruit, but I shall rob you of them."

Fourteen, miming the Emperor Octavian, approached the bed and carelessly tossed the gladius to the floor. "Know that your death was never my ambition, Cleopatra."

The pharaoh threw her head back laughing. Peaches' move was so good it might as well have been a toxin-induced muscle spasm. "No? And I thought the snake was the most venomous animal in my chamber," she sneered and lifted herself up. A firm body slipped from the soft fabric, covered only by thin gold chains and colorful gems. Octavian recoiled involuntarily as she spread her arms and her legs. "Mount Egypt's throne, Caesar, as long as you can."

He shook his head. "You are insane, Pharaoh."

Cleopatra cunningly bowed her head. "And you are the virtuous general? You knew what would happen when I sent your praetorians away. You saw the scribes and the maids come here and receive final orders. Do not pretend that you did not know that today you would see me breathing for the last time. The two dead guards at my door are futile victims of your madness."

Octavian raised an arm. "Silence! You are dying, and the poison is clouding your senses."

Cleopatra grabbed his arm and pulled him into bed. "Morituri te salutant, Caesar."

Peter bent over Luisa and kissed her passionately. She returned the kiss with a groan, and a few seconds later pushed him away playfully. He sat up and looked into his lap. He was already hard. Luisa lowered her head and put his cock in her mouth. Peter sighed. She even treated him to some of the wonderfully nasty sucking sounds that drove him crazy. He closed his eyes, only to find himself in Ms. Jana's office. The lips that caressed his glans, and the tongue that boldly ran over its tip was that of the out-of-this-world gorgeous lady of the house, rewarding him for a great website. His eyes quickly opened again, the inner betrayal and the guilty conscience born of it forcing him to do so. Luisa's head bobbed up and down in his lap. Her beautiful body swayed with her movement, and he placed a hand on her back.

"Enough," he murmured helplessly, "Or I'll… uh…"

She released his cock and lay back, legs spread. Peter brushed the covers fully aside and pressed his lips onto her thigh, sliding slowly up it. She misunderstood his ambition and stretched her leg, thinking he wanted to take her toes in his mouth. He grabbed her leg, heaved it to his opposite side and stared down at her lovely little cunt.

Luisa grinned. "Nice change of pace."

He just nodded and locked his abdomen with hers, her leg resting against his torso.

Octavian's strong hands gripped Cleopatra's hair and held her head. His large, fleshy penis rose to her lips and the pharaoh hesitated to open them. He snorted. "Cowardly until death, Queen of Egypt?" A few startled sighs escaped the audience. Cleopatra opened her mouth and let his cock enter. It was a slow, thorough penetration that strained her gag reflex and made her slender body tremble as she resisted it. His hands, however, prevented her from sucking his cock. What Octavian was doing was an invasion, the desecration of a temple, the filling of a queen's commanding mouth with the conqueror's cock. Instead of allowing her a relieving suck and lick, thus placing her humiliation in her own hands at least, he began to thrust. Cleopatra hummed in outrage. Octavian made no expression, but watched his shaft, streaked with thick veins, as it slipped from her plump lips and thrust inside again. Still, his movement was slow, deliberately degrading, possessive – more like language than sex. Cleopatra began to laugh, muffled. He scoffed, "The fact that you still manage to slip any sounds past my shaft is typical of you, Queen." She seized his hands on her head, and he let go of her hair. His cock drew long strings of saliva from her wide, strained mouth. "Beg me to finish it, Pharaoh."

She shook her head. "You'll have to come and get it, bastard."

Peter penetrated her and sighed instantly. "Oh, fuck."

She looked into his eyes, and he initiated a slow, tender rhythm. Luisa bit down on her tongue. Peter watched his cock enter and exit her tight vagina. Peter had no trouble getting aroused and making love to Luisa, but it usually required extensive thoughts of her feet at least, better yet if he could touch and taste them first. Luisa moaned sweetly and moved her abdomen, which he noted with fascination. Her erotic persona usually did not know such generosity, insisting on sexual service instead. She was genuinely pleased by this interlude, he concluded, and slowly increased his speed, contrary to the tingling, red-hot warnings of his nerve endings, which were racing toward climax in time-lapse. Luisa pushed him deeper inside with the leg he wasn't leaning against, and he actually moaned a helpless "Careful." She giggled and basked in his thrusts, stretching out her arms and making him almost come immediately by this unusual, ecstatic sight.

Octavian flung Cleopatra onto the mattress, turned her around with a strong grip on her hips, and ripped off her jingling, effete gold chains. The audience howled with excitement. His hands clutched her slender hips and lifted her up. His greedy, pulsing cock stroked her butthole a few times in blatant threat. Cleopatra moaned indignantly, and Octavian bent over her petite body and pressed her head into the mattress, silencing her. With a triumphant grin, he penetrated her cunt and announced, "This is mercy, Pharaoh. I will let your people know that your last word was my name screamed out with relish, and your last thoughts were of the relief of not getting my cock shoved up your royal arse." Cleopatra moaned a sound into the mattress that rang as outraged as it did lustful, and Octavian's first proper thrust turned it into a whimper. He laughed and repeated the single, brutal thrust. Her abdomen trembled beneath his force, and Fourteen knew how to position his own body so that the audience saw the reddened labia stretched to the extreme when he pulled his veiny cock from her, revealing telltale wetness. "It pleases you, Queen," he sneered and engaged in less brutal but regular thrusts, to which she responded with a shriek. Her fingers crinkled the white sheets, her head rose from the pillows, and her face was an almost worryingly contorted grimace of pleasure.

Luisa's breasts jiggled to their rhythm, and she squinted as he began to apply pressure to her mons with the flat of his hand. He honestly had little idea if this was actually doing anything, but at least he imagined it was increasing the sensation for her a little. Peter gazed at the ceiling rigidly for a few thrusts, thereby earthing his thoughts. His girlfriend spasmed; he clenched his teeth and kept up the speed she enjoyed. Luisa stuck out her tongue tensely, and he laughed gutturally, enjoying the rare sight of great pleasure on her face. Luisa came in an adorable squirm, and Peter cherished fucking her for a few moments more. He didn't presume to be able to cause multiple orgasms, but at least till his own climax came, he could extend her pleasure, touch her, and make her feel good.

Octavian took Cleopatra like a street whore. His disinhibited, thrusting abdomen suffused the theater with obscene clapping, and the empress roared her pleasure out in an animalistic voice. The pharaoh shook herself several times in raging orgasms that the warlord ignored. He withdrew from her at intuitive intervals to whirl her jaded, trembling body to other positions. She let it happen, once even reaching out in a tender gesture for his hand, which he struck out as casually as he did angrily. When her strength waned and he detected the snake's venom in her heart, he abruptly ended his act, demonstrating almost surreal self-control. Cleopatra breathed heavily, her tanned chest quivering. Octavian stepped around the bed and stroked her cheeks. "Beg for it." His moist, reddened cock hovered above her. She shook her dizzy head. He nodded in silent contradiction. Her lips trembled. Octavian gently touched them and opened her mouth with delicate force. "You want it." Cleopatra nodded imperceptibly and a last spark of hatred passed through her eyes. She opened her lips willingly and let Octavian's cock in, downright anticipating it. Her arm grabbed his hip for support. This time, he allowed her to suck and blow his shaft. He grinned at her triumphantly, her big brown eyes looking up at him. Her runny makeup drew lines of black across her face. "Enjoy it," he hissed, his voice as venomous as the snake's bite. "It took a Roman to make you happy in Egypt, Pharaoh." Her motions slowed, lazier, until the lips of Egypt's queen nearly detached from his cock. "Don't be so…" – he suddenly realized what was going on and seized her head – "You have the audacity to…?" Cleopatra didn't move. Without finding release, he stood over her flaccid body. Her lips freed his burning hot cock, and her arm with its betraying bites fell back onto the wrinkled sheets. Outside the door, the hasty footsteps of several guards rang out. The midnight blue curtain closed.

This white space demanded to be filled. It cried out for content. Peter bit his lip. He was no designer, but he had learned the basics of a tool used to create wireframes, the digital outlines of any modern website. So far, his sketch of the website for the ladies of the house contained only a flat rectangle with rounded edges that he used to symbolize a button. A button that led to the application. Ms. Jana had given him a few rudimentary conditions that applicants had to meet, but he could hardly create a form with "Have you failed at life in just the right way and yet face an obscure crisis of purpose of a sexual as well as emotional nature that can hardly be put into words? Yes/No?" He smirked softly, and Sandra shook her head as she entered the office.

"Your dominatrixes?"

He exhaled at her light joke. "Yes. *My* dominatrixes. I need more info, Sandra."

She snorted. "Scheduled a second meeting already?"

He shook his head. "They're waiting for feedback from me. It's definitely going to take more communication." At least a rough draft would work out. A succinct opening via an SEO-appropriate headline would greet the visitor, which would then be followed by a short text that had to hook the reader right away. *God*, thought Peter, the headline and introduction had to be masterful if this page was to even vaguely perform.

The text was succeeded by a striking, yet stylish button that would either open an email program or lead to a yet-to-be-created submission form that the user would have to fill out. Since the page seemed extremely lacking to him, he added a few large boxes filled with a stylized mountains and a sun symbol as placeholders for images. These could be removed if they did not appeal to Ms. Jana.

"I don't like it," Carlotta said, crossing her arms briskly and making an adorable pout. Michael looked down his naked body. He wore only the bright pink penis cage. Carlotta, whom he towered over about a head, was wearing even less. A stark naked, busty slave girl, smiling out from under a shock of flaming red hair, who had introduced herself as Cherry, had picked him up the day after the exciting theater performance and brought him to this modernly furnished tower room.

The room's occupant, a bubbly little blonde named Lady Carlotta, had greeted him completely undressed and grinning broadly. The entire room had been set up to be inhabited naked. The floor was covered with warm rugs; all the furniture had round corners; blankets and pillows were scattered everywhere. Carlotta kept a youthful style that vehemently contrasted the bombast of the rest of the house, yet had an exciting and regal young dignity all its own.

The slaves, usually lingering here as living furnishings, had been sent away before. Today, Carlotta was solely taking care of little Michael, who stood in the middle of this sort of dorm room that had been tweaked to blossoming erotica and blown up to immense size.

Carlotta was playfully pawing around and pondering, her bare soles making overwhelmingly erotic tapping sounds on the floor. "I'll set you free," she said, taking a small key from a pretty, industrial-style dresser. "I don't like these constraints."

Beneath his thrilled, thankful gaze, she opened the clasp of his penis cage, pulled off the top shell, and carefully fumbled his testicles out of the socket underneath. He peered at himself in disbelief and back up into Carlotta's broadly grinning, blue-eyed face. "Th-thank you."

She winked and tossed the plastic device over her shoulder. "No worries, Mikey. I think all dicks should be free. Don't you?"

He didn't quite know how to respond to that and shrugged blandly. "Uh, yeah?"

Carlotta smirked and moved closer. "Did you like how I shoved my ass in your face

on your first day?"

He nodded. "Yes, Mistress Carlotta."

She winked and pinched his nipple. "You little perv."

He reflexively reached for his nipple and returned her friendly smile. She shook her head affectionately and touched his penis, rubbing his glans between her thumb and index finger, to which he responded within a few seconds. He sighed softly at this hint of release, this suggestion of eruption. Carlotta's other hand stroked his cheek. She continued her touch until he was fully erect and eventually wrapped her hand around his entire shaft.

"You're a grower, so cool," she said. "I usually have the fleshy ones, but every once in a while, one of those does the trick. The fleshy ones are big already and get just a little bit bigger when erect. The growies like you are more like little twinks when flaccid" – she explained this all with the naïve demeanor of a young girl doing a sex ed assignment – "but grow much more when they get hard and… are often even harder than the fleshy ones." She could have been telling him anything right now. Michael nodded with his mouth open.

Carlotta gently pulled on his cock. "Come," she demanded, leading him around the room by his penis as if on a leash. "I wanna know exactly what you're about."

Michael was allowed to lie down on a slim piece of furniture, the head end of which curved upward to raise his torso a few degrees. It deliberately played on the "psychiatrist's couch" cliché, and he placed his arms in his lap uneasily while Carlotta stood beside him. He saw everything of hers. The cute little crease between her slender legs, the small breasts, the large, adorable navel. Her dainty feet made pitter-patter steps on the floor, and her almost white-blonde bob punctuated her gestures.

"Michael," she purred, leaning down to give him a girlish, quick kiss on the forehead, "Why do you like dominant women?"

He was still erect, looking into her cool eyes uncertainly. "I-I can't explain it well."

She played with her tongue in her cheek. "Well, it doesn't have to be explained well. Honest will do."

He laughed uncertainly. "Uh. I've always liked dominant women, actually. Ever since I was… ever since sexuality was a thing. So… early adolescence? Yes. I'm attracted, I think, to the idea of giving up control. Putting yourself in the hands of another person. It's a lot about trust," he said softly, pointing to his erection in embarrassment.

Carlotta whistled, impressed. "Wow, did you read that off the Tinder bio of a female 'Fifty Shades of Grey' fan?" The sarcasm was impossible to miss, and he had to laugh out loud at himself. Her slender belly twitched briefly before she snorted and sheepishly put her hand over her mouth.

"Sorry, yes," he concluded, looking up. "That did sound like a generic explanation."

She nodded and brushed his cheek. "I know this is difficult to answer, but I want you to try. What makes you happy about the thought of belonging to a woman?"

He took a deep breath. She watched his blond mop of hair and almost thought she saw the little cogs rotating behind his forehead.

The result of his reflections was a single word: "Pride."

She winked. "I like that. Pride in the woman you serve, or pride about the opportunity to serve?"

He furrowed his brow and shook his head. "Not in that way. Pride over the recognition a lucky woman would give me."

She caressed his chest. "Good boy."

Michael looked up at her. Carlotta grabbed his hand and placed it on her hip. He had earned the right to fondle her bottom. "I like when women laugh," he whispered. "It's nice to be around them when they're happy. I like being the center of their attention," he admitted, ducking his head guiltily. "Sounds really selfish now that I'm saying it out loud." She shook her head, allowing the probing movements of his hand. "So I like dominant women," he concluded, "Because they know how to make themselves happy, and they get that happiness preferably with me or through me."

Carlotta winked. "What games should a dominant woman play with you? In an entirely sexual sense."

He smiled and looked up at her slender, petite body. "I like to be used for pleasure. When she enjoys letting off steam on me. I like to massage and kiss feet. I like to cook."

She smiled and, taking a big step, stepped over him. "Cooking! Very sexual, Michael…" With legs wide, she stood over the couch, Michael gazing up at her. Carlotta leaned down and braced her hands against the backrest, to the left and right of his head. Her breasts formed sweet, pendulous balls over his chest. She stood, their bodies not touching. A wide grin crept onto her face. "How many women have used you for pleasure so far, Michael?"

He gazed stiffly into her eyes, his cock standing up erect, longing for the embrace of Carlotta's cunt hovering above him. "Just one. My girlfriend Elena, er, Lady Elaine."

Carlotta laughed amiably. "And still you know all these

things about your sexuality, Michael? How would you serve me? Tell me what an evening with my little slave Michael might be like."

"I would like to send you something," Peter said.

Jana looked through the round opening of her massage table to the floor. "Gladly. What is it?" Lilith held the smartphone to her ear while two other slave girls massaged the lady of the house. Her day had been exhausting, and she had decided to indulge in this mundane method of relaxation.

The spa area adjoined the house's indoor pool and sports area and was less well equipped than Jana liked. A cramped sauna with pale wood paneling that dated back to the 1980s, when the trend was gaining momentum, two massage tables and an empty room with yoga mats made up all the options the house had to offer. Jana wanted to invest, expand, and improve, but to do so, she needed marketable slaves. Handsome Fourteen was waiting for a buyer; numbers Fifteen and Sixteen had left the house on their own request, and Seventeen was still at the very beginning of his training.

"It's something called a wireframe," Peter explained, clearing his throat. "It's like a sketch of the website. A draft. I put it up with the information I got from our chat. With texts and placeholders. I would like to hear your opinion."

Jana understood. "With pleasure. Do I need a special program to view the wireframe?"

Peter laughed briefly. There was an unpleasant rustling in the connection and a soft crackling sound as he noted and corrected something. Jana became aware that he was talking through a headset. "No, no special program. I'll export it to you as a PDF and a JPG. Then you can decide."

Jana considered for a moment. "PDF."

He nodded audibly. "No problem, PDF it is. I'm not

sure about a few things though. As mentioned, the website seems vacuous."

Jana smirked toward the floor as the hands of two naked slave girls oiled and massaged her. Lilith's hand stoically held the smartphone. She let crafty Mr. Wartmann draw the conclusion himself and was thievishly pleased when he followed suit.

"I think a follow-up in-person appointment would be wise. Or several."

Jana hummed with delight. "I'd love to."

He sighed. "Since we have so little content, the text, above all, must be perfect. We need a really, really catchy H1 with the most important keyword. Plus, the little copy underneath and then – bang! – the button to apply."

Jana didn't understand every abbreviation, but she could roughly follow him.

"And," he continued, "It would make sense for us to make a decision between applying by email or by a form on the website. That's where I need your input. Should we decide to go with the form, what do we ask the visitor in it? Before this, as you know, the user made an important decision: 'Okay, I'm applying there. This totally appeals to me.' What comes next? Well, you had told me criteri—"

Jana giggled. "You're amazing, Mr. Wartmann."

His stream of words ended abruptly. "I beg your pardon, Ms. Jana?"

She registered his lovely choice of words with delight. "You are amazing," she repeated, feeling the warm fingers of an extremely talented slave sliding along her spine. "And I'm very glad you're helping our house."

He paused briefly, apparently about to laugh, but refrained. "Thank you."

She smiled with genuine sympathy. "You've earned it. I think you're the right man for this. I'm available on Monday."

"You're coming home, my Lady," Michael said

carefully.

Carlotta touched his nose with the tip of her finger. "'Carlotta,' please. I'm almost as young as you, honey. We can be on first name terms."

Michael smiled nervously. "You' re coming home. It's been a busy day. I'm waiting for you behind the door, and I'm all excited."

She lowered herself onto his stomach and fondled his chest. "What are you wearing?" The warmth between her thighs flowed onto his abdomen.

"Nothing. I'm completely naked. Just a collar with a pet name you gave me. You come through the door and smile down at me. I get to take your shoes off and…" She smiled broadly. He cleared his throat. "I get to take a… h-hrm… a very deep breath from the open shoes."

Carlotta stuck her tongue out cheekily. "Ah, I possess a naughty foot fan?"

He swallowed. "Yes. Then you put the leash on me, and I'll help you out of your jacket. I've cooked for us. Your plate and a glass of wine are already at the table. Mine is still in the kitchen, because you decide on the spur of the moment where and how I get to eat."

She nodded significantly and sank down full onto his belly. "Very wise!"

He was almost driven insane by the natural touch of her bare skin; her breasts pressed against his chest, his cock rubbing against her thighs. "Because I've been a good boy, I get to eat next to you at the table," he continued. "And you like the food." Carlotta rested her head on his chest and hummed her approval. "Later, you'll like a little entertainment, so you order me to get your favorite toy out of the closet. It could be a small paddle, a slim whip, or anything else we both enjoy."

Her hand went to his forehead and gave him a playful swat. "Dork. I obviously choose a wooden spoon for my little chef de cuisine."

Michael laughed. "Ah, yes! That would be great. So I'll

bend over the table to get my butt all exposed and as wide as I can." Carlotta snorted and nuzzled his throat as he continued to describe his humiliation with flaming red cheeks and words flowing faster and faster. "You praise me. Then I get to guess how many strokes I will receive. If I guess too low, you increase the originally intended number by ten. If I guess too high, you just take my number. I'm getting ready, and I have to concentrate on relaxing the muscles."

She kissed him on the chest and sighed. "Finger me, slave." He placed his hands in her lap. She purred, "Keep talking while you do it."

Luisa had not shopped for groceries, nor had she taken a few on-hand ingredients out of the freezer so they would be thawed by the time Peter arrived. She did, however, greet him with a kiss and very good spirits, a rare gesture, her form of praise, and at the same time, an almost cynical compensation for the fact that he was allowed to prepare dinner for her with leftovers, since she had not had the musings to do anything for the joint household today.

Peter went into the kitchen, scouted the refrigerator, and was quite confident he could whip up a meal for them both. He had no intention of making his quiet displeasure audible but asked in a forcibly aloof voice, "Was the store closed?"

No, of course the supermarket had been open at 4:30 p.m. on a weekday. However, he still wanted to know why she hadn't gone shopping.

"Huh? Nooo," she snarled from the living room, and Peter instantly sighed into the freezer, startled. Wrong question in the wrong tone of voice after a suspiciously good night's performance. He heard the soft thumping of her pretty little feet coming closer, and Luisa leaned into the doorframe of the kitchen. Her voice bristled with indignation. "We still have some of that corn I made."

No one would have let the two pale yellow half cobs in

the tarnished Tupperware pass as a meal for two healthy adults. Peter nodded. "Okay, then I'll make some of the fettuccine and the vegetable strips to go with it" – he smiled fondly – "so we'll have pasta-alla-leftoverroni?"

She nodded firmly and went back into the living room.

"I have to keep count of the strokes," Michael explained as two of his fingers curled and gently entered her vagina.

"Mmm," Carlotta sighed, snuggling against his neck.

"You take a few swings and make me wait for the first stroke. You're enjoying watching me twitch." She laughed softly and bit into his neck. His fingers started making small, rhythmic movements. "Then comes the first blow. I scream, a little frightened. The second blow. The third blow—"

Carlotta cooed, "You forgot to count."

He groaned, feeling his craving cock rubbing against her butt cheeks. "So you start from the very beginning, whipping me. I'm shaking with arousal."

Carlotta straightened up. "Go deeper, slave." He no longer had to press and uncomfortably twist his hand between both their bodies to penetrate her, and he tenderly guided both hands between her slender legs. Unfortunately, this upright sitting position, literally on his belly, deprived him of her touch on his rock-hard cock.

"You're giving me twenty-six strokes because I guessed that much. After that, I finally get to kiss your feet. You're wearing thin nylon socks that smell wonderful." She sighed as he found a depth and rhythm she liked. Michael maintained this, his tendons starting to show at the wrist. "You sit down for this. I'm on my knees in front of you with a sore ass and still shaking all over."

She squealed, "You have to ask for it!"

He nodded. "I'm begging you to let me kiss your feet because I'm so grateful for the punishment. Because I'm so happy you're here." She slowly laid her head back as he pleasured her. Her hands clamped down on his chest. She was using him completely, letting his hands guide her closer and closer to climax. Her voice faded into a thrilling, staccato whimper that nearly drove him insane. She sounded like an adult performer, encouraging his pulsating fingers. Moisture surged toward him. "You permit it," he said, strained. "I lie on the floor in front of you and kiss your feet. You place one foot on my head while I kiss the other."

Carlotta put a hand over his mouth, bent down to him with a ferocious look, almost manic, and breathing heavily, flicked her finger.

Peter had tried to work magic and had failed miserably. He liked fried pasta, so he had wrapped the corn cobs in the fettuccine and tried to sauté both and serve them with crunchy strips of vegetables. However, the fettuccine kept unrolling and falling into the pan when he tried to flip the cobs. At least they could eat it.

Luisa had the audacity to be pissed off about this poor treatment of her corn on the cob as well. "You have eustress," she said, chewing. Peter looked up. "It shows. You're in such a high right now because you have responsibilities, and you're in charge of a lot of Christian's decisions. Hence, also…" She winked meaningfully.

He smiled thinly. "I think so. However" – he lowered his fork – "I always love you. And I love you dearly, Luisa. I am, I think, not one of those people whose behavior off the job is strongly influenced by the stress during the job. I… I had a great desire for sex."

She smiled almost defensively. "Wasn't to say you're rarely up for it otherwise." She managed to talk to Peter about sex without saying "sex" or "making love" or "sleeping together" or anything else. Not for the first time, he envied her shrieking girlfriends the privilege of being allowed to say "fuck, screw, blow" in a conversation with Luisa without constraint. He was aware that he was being interrogated. She was investigating the causes of his eruption of lust. She was irritated; after all, coitus had occurred without him begging to initiate it with a foot massage.

"Point taken," he replied, sucking strips of carrot through his lips like short spaghetti. "But the stress is quite manageable, to be honest. A few strange new customers and a lot of explanatory phone calls, that's all."

Luisa tilted her head and said ironically, "Phone calls and new clients – things right up your introverted alley, honey."

They both laughed at this truth.

A door behind the strange psychiatrist's couch opened, and Carlotta fixed on the new person slowly entering. Her hand kept Michael's mouth shut and also prevented him from simply turning his head to see who was approaching them. Carlotta nodded in acknowledgement as the person came closer and lifted her abdomen from Michael's belly. Moisture dripped down her thighs and Michael's wet hands slipped impotently from her throbbing, hot little cunt.

The new person was a giant, muscular man, clad only in an embarrassingly small pair of mustard-colored panties. Michael's eyes wandered from the gigantic bulge in the tight panties to Carlotta's face. She laid her head back with a gasp of laughter and raised her chest. "Go on, Michael. Don't mind me."

He fell silent, uncertain. The guest with the face of a marble statue gazed stoically at Carlotta. Was he a slave, too? What was happening here? After all, she had been seconds away from an orgasm…

A slap in the face brought him back to the present. "Continue speaking, Michael." Carlotta's voice was cotton candy sweet to his ears, but her gaze was ice.

He gulped. "You're satisfied with my kisses, so I get to take off your first sock." She brazenly grabbed the hem of her visitor's panties and pulled them down. A cock of considerable size and thickness fell out, liberated, and slapped against the muscular man's thigh audibly.

"I'm lovingly setting the sock aside," Michael explained as Carlotta gestured toward the head end of the couch, nodding as the man stepped behind it. The thick glans hung half an arm's length above Michael's face. "You spread your toes," he said, and Carlotta's hands gripped the cock above him. Her slender fingers seemed obscenely small as they wrapped around the fat shaft.

"Do you worship me, Michael?" she asked, looking deep into his eyes.

He nodded. "I worship you."

When he finished the sentence, she took the stranger's cock in her mouth and gave such a pleased, delighted, almost relieved sound that Michael shuddered with envy and shame.

Actually, Peter thought, the ladies of the house were selling a crude kind of therapy. He had heard of a junkyard in Buenos Aires that allowed visitors to demolish broken cars with sledgehammers for a small fee. Most of the customers were jaded businessmen, marketing hotshots with frustrations over failed projects, and show-offs in midlife crisis. He frowned and stared at the TV, which was showing a series that Luisa found exciting. No, Ms. Jana's approach was not that crude.

"Don't wank," Carlotta barked hoarsely, letting the giant pick her up. Michael, meanwhile, sat upright and watched as the man effortlessly lifted the small woman and placed her on his stiff cock. She nodded to him, and he lowered her body to slowly enter her. She had her arms wrapped around his, and he was standing in the middle of the room holding the little woman in front of him like a large puppet with limbs. It didn't even cost him very much strength.

Carlotta glared at Michael. "Fuck me."

The giant started pounding Carlotta and the first penetration already made her shudder. Her high-pitched voice whined. She maintained icy eye contact with Michael. Obscene clapping sounded; Carlotta visibly struggled to keep her face from grimacing. The man fucked with the dismaying routine of a machine, and Michael envied his strength and the raw sexual energy he exuded.

Carlotta laughed brightly and, as the thrusts bobbed her up and down, continued to gaze fixedly into his eyes. "You can learn, Mikey," she moaned. "You – Ah! – you can be a good – Uh! – little toyboy for your lady – Ah! – your little Lady Elaine, if you want. Uh! I – a-Ah! – can show you how to – Mmmh! – how to fuck a girl, Mikey."

"Happiness," Peter whispered.

Luisa raised her head. "Huh?"

He waved it off. "Sorry, been thinking." She turned back to her series. Ms. Jana was selling happiness. Peter's brain was working at full steam, tying the ends of several threads together. He didn't have a real jumping-off point for the website's content yet, but at least he had a clue. The slaves are competent, intelligent people, but absolutely disoriented. His approach with the therapy had not been completely wrong but far too medical. The ladies of the house did not make knights in shiny armor out of lost causes, but carved rough diamonds and fashioned them into jewelry. Peter's thoughts raced as he realized the full extent of the training at Ms. Jana's house. Lives were turned upside down there; entire livelihoods wiped out and remade.

The giant folded and bent petite Carlotta as he pleased. She allowed every touch, laughing in disinhibition at the wet noises his fat, meaty cock produced in her tight cunt. "Stand up," she commanded Michael as the guy lifted her, stopping their act for a moment to fling her around and heave her into an even more degrading position. "Stand next to us and watch. You have to learn."

Michael stepped cautiously closer. The giant grunted harshly and maneuvered Carlotta toward a dresser, whose edges she clung to. He lifted her ass in the air and lowered it back onto his cock. When Michael appeared in the periphery of his field of vision, he thrust with great force. The veins in Carlotta's arms stood out as she clutched at the wood of the dresser. Even now, her slender, beautiful feet hung in the air. His hands held her by the hips, adding to the penetration with measured force. Michael imagined she felt his huge cock throughout her body. He watched as the hulking man fucked Carlotta almost senseless. Saliva leaked from her mouth as she turned her head to focus on Michael.

The guy grabbed her hair and pulled her head back. Her fingers and toes cramped, her legs wriggling around as if to kick at her tormentor. She finally came in a high-pitched scream of pleasure that went through marrow and bone and made Michael shudder. The giant deposited her almost carelessly onto the soft, carpeted floor and loomed above her. She nodded with a blank stare, her limbs performing languid, uncontrolled movements. He grabbed his wet cock and began rubbing it. He soundlessly and routinely brought himself to climax, went down on his knees and, with an almost inaudible groan, poured a considerable amount of cum into Carlotta's face, over her small breasts and navel. He pumped several times, gasping, and literally milked his cock empty over her body. Carlotta's little tongue thoroughly cleaned the thick rim of his glans of the last of it. He rose without a word, shoved Michael roughly aside, and disappeared.

"Finish your story of worshipping me like a goddess," Carlotta whispered hoarsely, running her finger through a thick drop of cum that had pooled between her breasts and putting it in her mouth. Michael remained silent. She looked up at him with raised eyebrows, sucking on her cum-stained finger like a lollipop. "Hello?! Ground control to Mister Small Dick…?" She purred, "I want you to tell me how you sucked my toes after I punished you with the wooden spoon. In case you lost your train of thought: I think I was just about to spread the toes for you…"

"No," Michael interrupted, startled by the force of his own voice. "Not after… after such a display." His thin back surged. He took a deep breath and demanded, "I want to put the penis cage back on and leave."

Carlotta smiled broadly. "Most interesting."

CHAPTER 4: L'APPEL DU VIDE

"Crows," Peter said, shaking Jana's hand. She didn't leave it at such a professional gesture and gave him the French bises, a breathy smooch on each cheek. Peter smiled in surprise.

She looked up in the air. "Crows?"

He nodded and cleared his throat. "Yes, I just thought a flock of crows would be a fine detail for the house. It would make the spooky look perfect."

Jana laughed wryly and braced her arms on her hips. "Ha ha, Mr. Wartmann."

He winked cheekily. "Just kidding. I must admit, though, that the atmosphere puzzles me. Try to put yourself in my shoes." They entered the entrance hall and turned toward the marble staircase that led to the administrative wing. "When you're here, you wonder what is going on behind these walls, in the basement, or in the next room," he elaborated, hoping not to offend her.

Jana winked. "Quite extraordinarily degenerate acts of decadence and perversion, of course, Mr. Wartmann. You should see the jizz fountain and the freshly trimmed Venus mound in the garden."

He nodded, chuckling. "I can't wait."

"Right now," Tatjana purred, circling Michael with slow steps, "Your adolescence is protecting you. You are healthy, slave."

Michael stretched his back. "Thank you, Mistress Tatjana."

The lady in charge of physical education wore white leggings, equally white sports shoes, and a red sports jacket that rustled softly with each step. Her black hair lay in a strict knot at the back of her head. She brushed his butt and flicked against the firm skin with a smirk. "But it will not always be like this. You're healthy because you're young. Three years at an office job and you'll feel the lack of back muscle" – her finger slid up his spine – "All it takes is one hell of a year of relationship crises, stress at work, job loss, fast food orgies, and you'll put on a gut." Michael swallowed quietly. "One too many parties with the wrong people, and you'll never get rid of smoking," she predicted.

He just nodded, though he would admit to more willpower than she was giving him credit for. He had been shooed out of bed early that morning by Cherry and escorted to the basement of the house. Michael had been afraid that his plain words to the frivolous Carlotta would have consequences, but a visibly good-humored Lady Tatjana had greeted him in a dressing room smelling of rubber abrasion and sent Cherry through another door with a snap of her fingers.

Now the black-haired Tatjana smiled broadly from her beautiful, tanned face with its deep dimples. "I have less than half a year to shape you, slave."

He cleared his throat. "I want to take full advantage of it, Lady Tatjana. Mold me."

She winked and bit her lip. "You'll regret saying that" – she gave him a smack on the butt – "But it was the right answer. On your knees."

Jana opened the door to her office, and Peter was pleased to see a LAN cable, a pot of coffee, and a second laptop, probably Ms. Jana's, on the table by the two seating pods.

"The Wi-Fi is only theoretically stable in this building. Plus, there are so many users," she said, pointing to the cable.

He took a seat and booted up his laptop. "Thank you." Jana sat down and crossed her legs. Peter typed in his password and looked at the little loading circle on the desktop. "Have you checked the wireframe?" he asked.

Jana nodded and opened her laptop in her turn. "I think it's very nice as a framework, but there are some rectangles below the button that I couldn't put my finger on."

Peter nodded and opened the slowly loading design tool he had used to create the wireframe. "Those are placeholders for images. I've put them in for the time being. If you don't like them, I can take them out again."

Jana hummed indecisively and leaned back. Her gaze locked on Peter, who smiled shyly. "The page could use a little jazzing up, couldn't it?"

He nodded cautiously.

"A wide screen – filling the whole display," she mused aloud, making a spacey gesture.

Peter smiled. "Good idea. It's better than the two little pictures I had in mind. But—"

Jana raised a finger with a grin, voicing what he was trying to politely paraphrase, "Too erotic a picture would, in turn, be counterproductive. We don't want to lure customers into a brothel. We want to attract promising raw material for the product portfolio."

Peter laughed silently and shook his head. "I'll never get used to talking about people like that."

Jana winked cheekily and flexed her foot. "You don't have to, Mr. Wartmann."

Tatjana put a collar on him and was visibly pleased to see it matched the color of his pink penis cage. He smiled self-consciously as she attached a chain to the eyelet of his collar and wound it up in her hand. "You don't have to lose weight," she murmured, running her hand over his belly the way one strokes the fur of a cute animal, "But selectively build up muscle. If we had more time, I'd set up a proper training and nutrition plan, but I won't make a Fourteen out of you in half a year. So we're going to train the major muscle groups sustainably." She tugged on his collar. "Come along."

On all fours, Michael followed her into a brick basement, where an array of sports equipment awaited their usage. She led him toward a large, state-of-the-art treadmill. "Warm-up first," she said, unhooking his leash.

He glanced up briefly to make sure he was allowed to stand up before stepping onto the treadmill. Tatjana whistled melodically for someone and plugged a small cable that connected a device the size of a flash drive into a vacant slot on the treadmill's control panel, where athletes would otherwise charge their phones.

The slave girl named Cherry came out of one of the archways and unrolled a soft mat in the middle of the room, as if she was going to do yoga. Tatjana pulled a small, oval device in pale pink from the pocket of her sports jacket. Michael raised an eyebrow. Cherry closed her eyes. Impossible to tell if she was afraid, excited, or relieved. Maybe all at the same time. Her skin was white as snow, the red of her long hair almost falling to her big, soft tits. A light blush formed in her cheeks and endearingly competed with her hair.

Tatjana clapped her hands together. "You two cuties are about to have a session of hot morning sex, orgasm optional."

"Aside from the pictures, I have a handful of content elements in mind," Peter said, enjoying the fact that Ms.

Jana had slid her seat next to his so he could just point to the relevant parts within the wireframe.

She nodded with a grin. "You bombarded me with lingo during our phone call," she admitted, stroking his upper arm, "But I'm an enthusiastic student, Mr. Wartmann. We need, if I interpreted your jargon correctly, a big headline, some stimulating body text underneath, and a snappy catchphrase for the big button that leads to the application."

He nodded with a smile. "Right. But before we get into that much detail, let's clarify whether we want to use a fill-in-the-blank form or have a big text box open up for free-form typing."

"Ah! I see. If we use a form, we have to provide questions for the fields: whys, wherefores, hows. Tell us something about yourself."

Peter nodded with a pinched face. "Here, I must confess, my area of expertise ends. If a form is required, you have to provide me with the queries. If you want me to develop it, I need more in-depth information about the men in question."

Jana sat back and looked thoughtfully into Peter's screen. "I think continuous text is more revealing. Answering questions tells me less about a person than a long, self-written paragraph."

Peter believed both options had their pros but would not contradict a customer request born from experience. "I'll note a large text box. A single question in the sense of 'Why do you think you'd be a good fit for us?' would still be necessary."

Ms. Jana typed something into her own laptop. "We can manage that."

"I'll help you, darling," Tatjana purred, slapping Cherry's bottom. Michael grew aware of Cherry's soft body, soft even for a young woman who legitimately could have called herself curvy. An adorable little belly bulged over her lap and her full hips quivered for another moment following Tatjana's slap. She was surely getting special attention from the athletic mistress.

Cherry spread her legs, and Tatjana reached into her lap and played with the little object on her rosy labia. "This little guy vibrates – on a low setting, mind you – as soon as sweet Michael over here reaches a certain speed. If you want to climax, Cherry, you'd better give your jock a good cheer. Lie down." She bit Cherry's neck lustfully, inserted the wireless-controlled vibrator into her, and the slave girl cheeped excitedly. Tatjana watched with a grin as Cherry lay down on the mat and then looked to Michael, her doe eyes wide.

"Are you waiting for a starting shot, slave?" asked Tatjana with raised eyebrows.

Jana rose and took a few steps. From the huge transom window behind her desk, warm sunlight fell on her face. Peter watched her with interest. They had just been talking about the headline and copytext when she got up to walk, thinking as she did so. He was waiting for the right moment to pitch his happiness-in-life idea to her.

Ms. Jana, as she stared thoughtfully out the window, was a dark silhouette against the glaring light, and Peter took the liberty of a quick glance down her slender legs. She wore light gray pants that seemed to have been excerpted from a full outfit in that color. A white top falling in cool folds left her slender arms bare. Braided leather cords dropped from the top's collar, held together at breastbone level by a silver clasp like those bolo ties in Western movies. Her feet – Peter made sure Jana was still looking out the window – were in open-heeled shoes with just two straps. A narrow one wrapped around her slender ankles; a wide one laid gently across the base of her toes. He bit his lip. She was wearing open-toed shoes for the first time, and Peter took a deep breath to maintain his concentration. Jana had slender, elegant woman's feet with a majestic arch that seemed to almost tauntingly resist touch with the insole of her shoes.

Carefully, Michael picked up speed. His footsteps plodded loudly on the sturdy rubber. Tatjana glanced back and forth between him and the tension-stricken Cherry. Michael felt the same way, for the slave girl was a feast for the eyes. Her green eyes gazed at him, and he thought he detected a faint nod. He sped up. Tatjana walked around Cherry with her arms folded behind her back and looked at her, smiling softly. When Michael began to jog, Cherry gave a startled sigh and her knees twitched for a moment. The vibrating little toy had begun its work. Michael caught Cherry's gaze again, and they reached a tacit agreement: *Stay just fast enough to keep the vibrator activated, and I'll somehow try to cum as quickly as possible.*

Michael had the fitness of a healthy young man who was largely taking care of himself, but who had no particular ambition in athletic matters. He was able to jog along like this for a while, but he already had to remind himself to breathe properly in order to prevent side stitching. Tatjana got rid of her sports jacket. A short top that left her taut belly exposed was revealed. Her breasts sat plump and firm in a sports bra, her muscular buttocks demanding maximum performance from the stretchy fibers of her leggings. Cherry sucked in a sharp breath and nodded to Michael. The latter returned the nod as a first drop of sweat trickled down his forehead.

"Anything along the lines of," Jana said cautiously, "'Everything will change for you from here on out'?"

Peter nodded slowly. "That's heading in the right direction for the headline. We need an 'umbrella' term though, a keyword to hang the whole page on. I can't run an analysis without knowing the core of the message we're optimizing for. I…" he hesitated. She turned and leaned against the windowsill. Peter sighed.

"Actually," he said, "You're helping two people at once. The man who becomes the product and leaves behind an unsatisfying life, and the woman who buys him. The bottom line" – he smiled shyly – "is that you are selling happiness."

Jana returned his smile and tilted her head. "I am?"

Peter simply nodded.

She pushed herself off the windowsill and came closer. Her heels tapped softly on the ancient parquet floor. Peter admired her slender toes for a brief moment, lifting from cute little beds in the inner sole, before looking up at her again.

Cherry put her hands in her lap, which earned her an admonishment in the form of a curt "Ah!" from Tatjana. With her hands flat on the yoga mat, she again sought eye contact with Michael, who, at the sight of the slouched, curvy beauty and the knowledge of Lady Tatjana's leering gazes, had to combat entirely different problems. He had an erection. His cock wanted to swell and pressed painfully against the pink plastic of his cage. The skin of the glans oozed unpleasantly from the opening that served him to go to the bathroom. He groaned in annoyance. The real pain would set in with a lag when his body realized he wasn't going to ejaculate and punished his testicles for it. To make matters worse, the painful erection made walking more difficult. Cherry whimpered.

Tatjana giggled and slapped his ass with the flat of her hand. "Are we exercising the minimax principle, darlings? Minimum effort with maximum result? I would, however, like to see a slave girl shrieking with pleasure and a slave gasping." She grabbed the small item on the treadmill panel and made an adjustment. "Now," she explained, "The intensity of the vibration depends on your speed, slave."

Jana sat down next to him again. "Happiness of life,"

she breathed softly. "That's a wonderful thought."

He tilted his head, goaded by her praise. "Thank you. When that idea came to me, it literally fell out of my mouth. Really puzzled my girlfriend when I sat on the couch and suddenly mumbled 'happiness' to myself."

Jana snorted. "Oho, got in a hassle?" Her cheeky wink challenged him further. He should have deflected, told her a little white lie, but he liked her. He enjoyed meeting her. If he was completely honest with himself, he had suggested this second meeting himself. What they were looking at here, side by side on two laptops, could have been an uncomplicated online or telephone conference. He wanted to be here, Peter realized, and decided not to lie to Ms. Jana. "No, there was no trouble. I was able to talk my way out of it. My partner, please don't take offense, Ms. Jana, would not be thrilled with this particular gig."

Jana nodded quietly. "I don't blame anyone for not being comfortable with the lifestyle of the residents of this house. However" – she stroked his arm again – "I'm uncomfortable with the idea that my inquiry is making you lie."

Peter shook his head, and there was more sadness in that gesture than he had intended to show. "Lying is not necessary. She's not even asking about it. I thought your very first email was an incredibly well-written joke and was about to tell her about it over dinner. 'Hey honey, today I got an email from some dominatrixes who want a website for a weird slave academy. Crazy, right?' Then I just kept quiet about it. She wouldn't have found it funny. The privilege of laughing with her at little innuendos is enjoyed exclusively by her terrible clique."

Michael ran. Lady Tatjana had challenged him, and he would not give in, would not become a disappointment, and would not become the target of her ridicule. Besides, who had ever made a woman orgasm by jogging? Cherry grimaced and, in appreciation, nodded in his direction. Her arms kept twitching upward, but she reminded herself not to assist with her hands.

Tatjana leaned over a barbell and looked over at them. "If endurance of the legs only were the endurance of the libido," she purred, winking at Michael, "A lot fewer people would be sexually frustrated. Unfortunately, it doesn't translate so easily int—"

Cherry unintentionally interrupted the mistress with a cute, pointed cry of pleasure. Michael was sweating profusely, but the sound of Cherry's pleasure released additional strength within him. With an animalistic grunt, sounding a bit feeble from his lanky throat, he increased the speed.

Cherry immediately raised a hand, her face a mask of sexual greed. "No-no," she cried, "Stay like that! Stay like that!" Tatjana laughed uproariously. Michael tried to restore the previous speed, and Cherry sighed gutturally. "A little faster, yes! …No, ah! Yes, like that!" The slave quivered, jammed her elbows into the mat and threw her head back.

Tatjana came closer and crossed her arms. Cherry bit her lip and looked at Michael. He felt her begging gaze as piercing as his lungs pleading for mercy, the pain of his pinched cock, and the churned contents of his stomach. His breathing had been accompanied by an involuntary panting for several minutes, and he rested his arms on the handrails to his left and right. His heavy footsteps throbbed on the treadmill's rubber mat, and Cherry screamed out her despair at having narrowly missed her climax. Michael returned the cry with a roar of frustration. Sheer instinct almost let him accelerate, but he maintained his speed, stared at the brick wall of this basement reeking of rubber abrasion, and ran.

Tatjana watched him with a proud smile. *Good slave.*

Jana closed her laptop and watched Peter Wartmann,

who had risen from his seat and was gesticulating with unexpected passion.

"I once told Luisa that the vending machine in the office was broken, and I had to get coffee for everyone from the mall two blocks away. On the way back, I slipped, seven paper cups in hand, bruised my hip, and burned my left arm with the searing hot coffee. You know what Luisa asked?"

Jana shook her head.

"She wanted to know how I knew how much sugar my coworker takes." Peter reached for his head and almost shouted, "Because I sit next to her all day, Jesus!"

Ms. Jana rose and put a hand on Peter's shoulder. "It was rude of me to ask you about private things. I went too far and made you angry."

Peter shook his head. "No, it wasn't. I-I came here angry. In fact, I have been angry for two-and-a-half years."

Jana sighed. "You should talk to your girlfriend."

Peter laughed cynically. "I can't do that anymore. In the night after our first appointment, there…" – he held his hand to his forehead – "Oh God, the things I blurt out just because someone asked with friendly, genuine interest. Sorry, I'm burdening a potential client of my employer with my personal problems, and therefore I should leave."

She held his arm tightly, and Peter was startled. It was not the surprising strength of her grip, but the sensation of force being wielded against him that astonished and almost made him shiver. Jana shook her head. "You don't burden me. I like you, Mr. Wartmann. You have a bright mind. You flourish when you talk about subjects that excite you. I would be very upset if a colleague of yours took over, and I had to forgo talking to you."

Peter was silent for a long moment before saying, "You haven't even been given a preliminary contract to sign. If I leave – and I should – no other web specialist will take over. The project is a semi-official running gag around the office that only a coworker in the performance division and I take seriously. 'Pete and his dominatrixes, ha-ha-ha,'" he said dryly, exhaling slowly. "Luisa and I had good sex," he continued his recount with a bitter laugh. This gig had just died due to his lack of professionalism – who cared what else he told Ms. Jana? "This is what happened after our first date. I was sexually loaded, and I was downright devouring my girlfriend. Without" – the bitter, terminal smile widened and became even more cynical – "...without having to ask her to put her feet in my face first, like some freak who can't fuck without having his disgusting fetish serviced first."

Jana tilted her head with a sad look. "That prevents you from talking to your partner?"

Peter nodded and cleared his throat. "Luisa is beautiful. But very demanding. I took the position at Web Specialists because she found her dream job in the city. I cut ties with a lot of friends because they bring out the worst in me. Now I am a big fish at a small agency. We live comfortably. Very expensive, but I can afford it."

Jana sat down and looked up at Peter.

He sighed. "Luisa is stunning. I'm the happiest man in the world when I'm close to her. That's why I put up with her idiosyncrasies. Her jealousy, her disregard for my interests. She handles my... my sexual *thing* well and doesn't make me feel like it's really weird. She is good to me and shows great tolerance. I repay her by being the best man I can be for her. That includes paying attention to her feelings, respecting her as a woman, and listening to her. She doesn't want to talk about things like this. If I told her about this project, she would draw the obvious conclusion and would be hurt to learn that my desire that night... came from here. Especially since she considers my preference to be..." – he gestured to the surroundings – "from *this* sphere. Pardon the word, but 'pervert' stuff."

Michael struggled with his arousal, his stamina, and Tatjana's sardonic looks. Cherry gasped, but nodded steadily, as if there was someone hovering in the air above her, whom she very clearly agreed with. His speed was right. Her small fists pounding on the yoga mat, she screamed. Tatjana watched as the slave's soft body shook in a blissful spasm. Cherry hummed helplessly. "I, ah! I have come, Lady Tatjana," she announced in a husky voice.

Tatjana abruptly pulled the little stick out of the treadmill's console. "Bravo, slave," she purred. Michael looked at her. Sweat trickled from his brow. She nodded in acknowledgement, and he finished his run. He wouldn't have lasted much longer and let the remaining momentum of the treadmill push him backwards before jumping off the device.

Cherry was breathing as heavily as Michael, and the two exchanged a fraternizing look.

Tatjana clapped her hands together. "Ahh, you two are so cute!" She sent Cherry away with a wave of her hand. "To your room, Cherry. Hop hop." The slave obeyed instantly and rolled up the yoga mat. Michael braced his arms against the wall and breathed extensively. "Drink," Tatjana hummed, holding out a bottle to him. He accepted it and looked uncertainly at the mistress for a moment. She snorted. "I'm not a jerk, slave. It's water." He took a sip and thanked her. As his breathing calmed, he emptied the bottle completely. Lady Tatjana nodded affirmatively. "Not the worst case I've ever had." He got down on his knees, resuming the starting position of the slaves in this house.

"I thank you, Lady Tatjana. That was an exhausting, but also an exciting lesson."

She petted his head. "It was a test. You are driven. I like that." She winked and gently slapped his wet butt. "Go take a shower, slave."

Jana's jaw nearly dropped through the antique parquet floor to the salon below as Peter poured his heart out to her. "Mr. Wartmann," she said, taking a deep breath, "There are a hundred objections buzzing through my head, which I would like to hurl at you at full volume. From the fact that making a partner submissive by means of his sexuality is a form of abuse, to the fact that a foot fetish is absolutely wonderful and a great thing, to the statement that you seem to invest much more in the relationship than your partner. Healthy relationships" – she rose, her gaze full of warmth – "don't work like vending machines into which you toss romance coins until eventually a fairytale wedding falls out at the bottom."

Peter was silent.

Jana leaned forward, and the wild brown of her eyes became rich and full like fertile earth. "Talk to her. I am fond of you, Mr. Wartmann. Please don't let yourself be hurt any further." He wanted to decline, but her index finger settled on his lips. "I'll accept the wireframe, as long as you add the idea with the widescreen. You send me the preliminary contract, I'll sign. You'll get an email from me soon – for I know who could help us find the right words."

Peter Wartmann nodded imperceptibly and drew in a heavy breath.

Ms. Jana smiled tenderly. "I look forward to our next appointment."

He didn't want to go home. He was afraid of what he was about to do, afraid of taking Ms. Jana's advice. If he screwed up, his relationship would end today.

His colleague Sandra had taken a call for Peter from Christian, the deputy director of Web Specialists, and left him a note. "Call Christian: Don't do dominatrix site / bad industry. Red light is for shitshow agencies."

Peter snorted. Christian had checked the emails during his vacation. "I swear," Peter had once said to Luisa, "If I have to commit to a *joint solution* with Christian one more time, I'll puke on his process-optimized patent leather shoes." That line of his had her really, genuinely, laughing out loud at the time. It had been a cute outburst by the self-controlled Peter, who was annoyed with the ambitious agency manager.

He put his laptop in the docking station and looked out the window into the swap-out pedestrian zone of this swap-out city. The curious thing was that Christian's ploys worked most of the time. Peter had no problem addressing hopeless endeavors with a client. Some things just didn't work. In such cases, Christian spoke of Peter as "our genius who wants to be pampered" and laughed at the eager optimizer whose clever analyses had failed alongside the client. "Look," Christian then told them, "We may have laid the wrong groundwork here. How about we challenge the idea again properly." And he succeeded. The agency depended on this stalwart soul. Failure did not exist, only "key learnings" and trial and error. Peter slumped in his office chair.

Christian's discipline for checking his emails had given him an opportunity to avoid the unpleasant conversation with Luisa. He would have to write a letter of refusal to Ms. Jana with a heavy heart, but that would be less hurtful than jeopardizing his relationship with his girlfriend on the advice of a dominatrix. He stared at the black screen and rolled the piece of paper with Christian's instructions between his fingers. Ms. Jana's words had stirred him. He smiled sadly into his dark office. "You can be charmed with sexy shoes and a few little words of praise," he mocked himself.

Perhaps Ms. Jana had tapped into a part of his personality that wanted more frequent and greater praise and attention. Had he been in such need of a friendly, *willing* touch on his arm and kind words? And she did claim that his sexual leanings were wonderful. She probably had to say that by default of her job, didn't she? Imagine a dominatrix rejecting a fetish! Then there was the assertion that Luisa was actually abusing him. Peter tossed the note across his screen to Sandra's side of the office and heard the rustle of the trash bin behind her empty chair – bull's-eye.

The feeling of shame over his sexual deviance was fighting a battle against the otherworldly elation that Ms. Jana had instilled in him. He had given up wishing for a normal sexuality and treated his fetish like an undesirable animal. Like a spider that dwelled beneath his clothes, pouncing on any unsuspecting partner with venomous fangs at the moment of peak intimacy, he craved touches of the most impossible parts of the human body. Luisa had come to terms with this. She tolerated the fat, hairy spider beneath Peter's clothes and knew how to feed it routinely when it cried out for its disgusting nourishment. Could he ask for more? Apparently, yes. This sacrilegious thought countered the decades of conditioned shame and restraint that had become a part of his character.

He thought now, of all times, about the anchorman of a late-night show who hosted an actress as a guest some time ago. She had emerged from backstage under the groovy tones of the studio band, and he praised her great outfit. When the camera panned down her dress toward her shoes, the actress burst out laughing, "Stop, no! Don't film the feet!" The host immediately echoed, "Oh, are the foot fetishists on your tail again?" She scoffed, "I swear, I could sell my worn shoes by the hundreds as often as they chat me up." The moderator indulged in a few distasteful jokes about "driving up the price with a cleverly placed piece of stinky cheese in the shoe" and "getting rid of grandma's old medical slippers for a profit this way." The audience roared with laughter, and Luisa changed the channel in embarrassment.

"Then we'll gladly pass," Janice said, a slicing gesture emphasized her statement.

Tatjana sadly weighed her head on her shoulders. "I

think that's a bit rash."

Carlotta stomped on the floor with cute anger and chirped, "We knew from the beginning that we had special requirements. It's a pity that in Mr. Wartmann, of all people… We met someone with… well… with *what*, actually?"

Janice snorted. "With a syndrome called acute ball-lessness, my dear."

Lady Derya, the maîtresse de cuisine who rarely spoke up, cleared her throat. "Carlotta is right. We knew of our requirements. Perhaps we underestimated what this task would do to someone who didn't know our way of life."

Janice rolled her eyes. "Derya, hunny, all we wanted was a website, and the contractor is incapable of providing it. Period. Full stop. The fact that the web specialist is bringing his own problems here and confessing that he screws his manipulative girlfriend better after five minutes of sweet talk from Jana is a side note of no fucking importance. Except that we should charge him for it as a therapeutic service." The inner circle of the house erupted in laughter.

Jana put her hand over her mouth. "Ladies, please." The women were slow to calm down.

Selina crossed her arms. "We haven't signed a contract or transferred any money yet. That's advantageous now that we are discussing whether to discontinue it. From another perspective, a person like Mr. Wartmann also is a stroke of luck for us. I wouldn't undervalue the service he has provided so far."

Jana had summoned her staff to her office to discuss her appointment with Peter Wartmann. She owed her ladies the truth about how the project had progressed so far. Her account of Mr. Wartmann's personal confessions had caused confusion, anger, and amusement. One detail in particular, blurted out rather incidentally by Mr. Wartmann, had raised tempers.

"Jana," Janice said imploringly, "He admitted that he

thought our inquiry was a joke. Only he himself and one other colleague are taking us seriously. Even if I leave out his personal problems, it's still absolutely dubious."

"Carlotta," Janice continued, "Correct me if I'm wrong, but a website like this isn't good *forever*, is it? We will have to work with Web Specialists for a long time if we settle for them. If only Mr. Wartmann and one other person there can deal with us as clients, we've made the wrong choice."

Jana nodded seriously. A very good argument by her domina.

"Right," Carlotta said, "But they can give us access to the website as well. It's not rocket science to revamp a headline and copy if need be. At least, I don't think it is."

Jana had flipped over one of the screens on her desk and opened the wireframe. In general, the ladies liked the simplicity of Mr. Wartmann's design. Jana watched her key ladies closely. Carlotta was furious at Janice's decisiveness and told her in a shrill voice that she was just hastily drawing a line in the sand. Tatjana cast uncertain glances at Selina, who in turn was eyeing Jana. Derya gestured at the screen and tried to make it clear to Janice, amid Carlotta's angry chirping, that any changes might be easy to apply if the page consisted only of a text-picture-button combination.

"I think," Jana whispered, and there was silence within the blink of an eye, "Mr. Wartmann is the right man for the job." Janice rolled her eyes. Jana turned in her direction, letting faint displeasure be heard in her voice. "Objections?"

The dominatrix proudly cocked her head. "I've said my piece."

A grin, the wonderful wickedness of which only women of the ilk of the ladies of the house could produce, crept into Jana's face. Her wide-falling curls seemed to literally twitch at these words. "Excuse me, but you haven't understood my decision yet, my dear."

"Luisa, I want to tell you about a rather special gig at the agency I've been working on for the past two weeks. It's nothing major – literally just one single site – but I know you won't approve of its nature. It's important to me to talk about it."

Luisa rose from the sofa. "Okay…?" She zipped up her cardigan and crossed her arms just below her chest as if she were freezing.

Peter was bothered that his well-formulated, diplomatic opening was only answered with an "okay" and what seemed like a preemptively woeful gesture. Her body language betrayed her. It annoyed her that he wanted to talk to her. He looked her in the eye, and Luisa must have sensed his displeasure because she stepped closer and brushed his collar. It was a mechanical motion, seeming almost rehearsed, as if she had reminded herself that she should occasionally express affection for her partner. Peter took a deep breath. "Actually, it's not a big deal at all, but my silence has made more of it. I know you're uncomfortable with this kind of topic, so I'll keep it short. I'm currently working on a site for a group of women – dominatrixes, actually – who run a kind of 'training center' for men who are sold as" – he formed quotation marks to the left and right of his head with both index and middle fingers – "*slaves* to rich women."

Luisa frowned, asking questions he hadn't seen coming. "How? Isn't that illegal? Isn't that human trafficking? How can a company like that even exist?"

Peter shook his head. "The men are practically dissatisfied people and… It's more like a permanent stay in some kind of BDSM-hotel for them. Then, at the end, they can be auctioned off in some kind of huge role-playing thing, at least that's how I understand it. It's actually a very peculiar form of a dating service."

Luisa nodded with a furrowed brow. "And they… want search engine optimization from you?"

Peter cleared his throat. "A complete website. The client is concerned with targeting the right men. It's to avoid being mistaken for a regular dominatrix establishment, or a brothel, sex store, or anything else along those lines."

"Where is this company?" she asked, and her confusion was complete. Something was stirring inside her. He had poured the information into her mind like a chemical, awaiting its reaction with the elements already inside the test tube. Luisa was not an impulsive person. She would thrive on this. He would have to work a long time to make up for this mistake if she *decided* to get angry.

"North of Clarke-Ring, at the very top."

She raised her brows imperceptibly. "You were there?"

Peter cursed himself for falling into this trap. "Yes," he admitted. "Twice for a client appointment. Last week and today."

As if all the pieces of a puzzle were falling into shape for his girlfriend in a split second, she turned away. "I see. Hence the… yeah. I see," she repeated, taking a deep breath. "I know you well enough to know the answer, but just because you're talking so bluntly all of a sudden, I'm going to ask the question anyway. Did you partake in anything and cheat on me?"

He shook his head. "No. I could never do that. I just wanted to tell you that there was this job."

She sighed. "There *was*?"

Peter smiled apologetically. "Yes. I had a note on my desk earlier. Christian checked his email on vacation and saw the inquiry from the ladies. He doesn't want to accept it."

Luisa concluded in a blink, "But you've had two meetings with the *ladies* without his knowledge?" She literally snotted the term in his face. Her voice gained sharpness; she had dissected the content of Peter's statements enough to now raise its individual parts against him like weapons.

Peter nodded. “Yes.”

She puffed out her cheeks and exhaled in frustration. “Wow.”

He raised his hands. “It was a professional query. I handled it professionally as Christian’s second-in-command. The site would have been super simple and doable in a week.”

She gulped. “That’s not the point, Peter. The point is that you took on the task in the first place, that you didn’t think to delegate it to a colleague, which a second-in-command might very well do, right? You could have brought it up for discussion in the morning meeting, but no. And two appointments with them, too? You, of all people, who would normally prefer to hide inside his laptop when a client shows up in person. Sure, Christian wasn’t there, and you had to take appointments by necessity, but two in-person meetings for a – as you said yourself – super simple site?”

He couldn’t argue with that because it was the truth. He had wanted to see Ms. Jana a second time and had enjoyed the first meeting as well. “Yes, two appointments.”

Luisa raised her arms in bewilderment. “Uh-huh, were there nice dominatrixes for you to gawk at then?”

He shook his head. “No, they were strictly business meetings, like I said,” he meekly returned. Luisa might even have believed him, but she had to vent her anger.

“Of course,” she sneered, elongating, “My boyfriend, who has an unnatural foot fixation, accepts an assignment by dominatrixes and meets with them twice without telling me. On top of that, he accepted the assignment on his very own and now that he has to step back from his pervy little plan because his superior is legitimately not keen on a whore site, he feels comfortable telling me about it.”

Peter was woefully silent. She had given the expected reaction, and he could literally see the balance of his account dwindling away in her mind. He had made a big mistake in hiding the matter. Luisa raised her hands demandingly. "Hello? Nothing to say?"

Peter shook his head.

She snorted. "Typical. Do you know what kind of a betrayal that is? I go out of my way to deal with your affections," she began to enumerate, and Peter felt a twinge in his heart at that word that wasn't there before. "I tolerate that you don't exercise that much, take rather mediocre care of your clothes and appearance, and defend you in front of everyone when they tell me that I could have done better. I listen patiently to your optimization babble. I realize you have a sexual problem, but it was irresponsible – to me – of you to even consider such an assignment." She tossed her hair back and said, "It's going to take me a while to trust you again, Peter. This secretiveness is a new facet of you, and I have to worry about what else your affections might do."

What she meant, however, Peter understood, was, *You will have to buy my amour again. I chose this quarrel because it gives me a chance to get even more comfort.* Her words hurt him. He knew he devoted significantly more to their relationship than she did and now felt, as strange as it sounded, anger at the disregard for the sacrifices he had made. "I'm supposed to be grateful that you're not replacing me?"

She hissed, "No, you're supposed to be grateful that I don't listen to the voices that tell me I'm out of your league."

He asked a question as simple, as logical, as it was drastic, "Why do you hang out with people who talk about me like that?"

She opened her mouth in an accusatory O and threw her hands in the air, completely flabbergasted. "That's the way women talk among each other, Peter. Do you want to be offended about that? Good morning, Mr. Wartmann, women gossip about their partners!"

He shook his head calmly. "No, I'm offended that you take my presence as a burden. I'm saddened that your sympathies come at a price. Do you actually notice how many of the things you take for granted that I lack? I no longer have friends to talk to about my relationship or about sex. I have my work, but you care very little about it. Didn't you just say 'optimization babble'? I do take care of myself, wear good clothes, and I am well groomed, because I know that's important to you. I pay more than three quarters of the rent for this translucent glass box of an apartment. I memorize silly details about your girlfriends to please you. Your coworkers literally kiss you goodbye, and I try my best to know as little about mine as possible because even the slightest mention of their names triggers an interrogation by you. You rely on your oh-so-exhilarating presence to make up for your toxic behavior, but the math doesn't add up by a long shot. You're quick to wield my foot fetish against me like a weapon, reminding me with gestures and words that it makes me some kind of freak. But, honestly, as uninvolved as you lie around doing *the starfish* during sex, a foot fetish is sorely needed to even be able to get it up."

Her gaze went blank. "I. Am. Your. Girlfriend. You dumbass! If you keep talking that misogynistic shit, I'm packing my bags."

He shrugged. "And where will you go? You can't even afford half the rent."

CHAPTER 5: HUMILITY

Luisa's departure hurt Peter as much as it relieved him. The grief he felt over the big fight and the more than uncertain future of their relationship was counterbalanced by a strange feeling of ease. He had liked to think of his love for Luisa as climbing a mountain, at the top of which absolute – actually, fairy-tale – happiness awaited. The disappointment of being deprived of the challenge of the ascent now seemed less terrible to him than the prospect of never reaching the summit, or of reaching it only after a complete transformation of his personality. He became aware of almost haunting details of his home and behavior that existed only because of Luisa. This wasn't about superficial things like furniture or decoration, but very subtle evidence of the self-effacing devotion with which he had showered his girlfriend. The first day after their argument, he came home with a big, fat kebab oozing with creamy yogurt sauce. He had not eaten such heavily fragrant dishes in the apartment before. Not because Luisa had anything against kebab, but because he suspected that the scent would bother her in the apartment. They had never discussed this, but Peter had been convinced of it. So he sat in his modern glass apartment and toasted the lights below him with a plastic bottle.

"I still don't like this dump," he said. While he ate, he flicked on the only lamp he had been allowed to buy when he furnished his apartment. Its overlong neck was flexible and reached almost every corner of the living room. When he was smart about it, the shade hung over the sofa in such a way that it reigned over the room like the futuristic equivalent of a chandelier. He delighted in his little light, burped loudly, and accidentally dripped a bit of yogurt sauce on the dining table.

Michael trembled. Kneeling on the floor, he listened to the approaching footsteps. High heels clicked on the black stonework of the corridor that led toward his guest room. The ladies used to have the thinly clad slave girls fetch him at specific times and bring him to them when it was his turn. Today, so Cherry whispered, he would be Janice's. And she'd come for him personally. When he fell out of the black suitcase into the heavens, Janice and Jana had been the first to greet him at the house. Janice was the – he may never tell her so – oldest of the ladies. The slaves called her the "Domina," which surprised Michael. In his estimation, all the mistresses of the house were dominatrixes, right? He assumed this short form was an honorary title since Janice seemed to be entrusted with particular tasks. The slaves reported damages to her, submitted bills from suppliers, picked up assignments, and ran quite mundane, out-of-game errands for her around town. Michael believed her the proverbial right hand of Ms. Jana. Her footsteps were drawing nearer.

Christian returned from vacation. Peter opened the glass door to his office and greeted his superior with a broad smile. "Back already? Didn't fancy a sabbatical?"

Christian laughed at the teasing remark. "Sorry, Peter, you'll have to come to terms with me, I'm afraid. That said" – he pointed to his clean, tidy desk – "I'm right back.

You want to onboard me for a minute?"

Peter nodded sagely. "Nothing special happened, to be honest. The medieval history park is almost finished. They are still missing a landing page for the windmill they're building. I was skeptical, but if we optimize more toward 'traditional milling,' 'history of baking,' et cetera, instead of 'life of a miller,' it has more potential. I can send you the analysis."

Christian grinned mischievously. "Starting your report with the ol' middle-aged theme park for grandmas and grandkids? Come on, what was up with those ladies of the house? I hear you already had a wireframe set up?"

Her heels came to a stop with a coarse crack, several feet from Michael's bedroom door, judging by the sound. The unmistakable thwack of a face slap rang out. Someone hissed painfully. A voice humming with ill-concealed malice said a single word, raising the last syllable to a question. "Michael?" The anxious, trembling voice of a young girl answered, "O-over there." She must have been pointing to his door. Michael froze instantly, for the girl had made a fatal mistake. As expected, a second slap echoed. "Over there. And further?" the voice dictated. The girl sniffled painfully. "The slave named Michael resides in this room, Lady Janice." The heels continued on their way without another word. Two slender shadows loomed in the narrow gap between the door and the floor. Michael preemptively cleared his throat.

"Yeah," Peter said slyly, "I had a wireframe and the client liked it. I stopped working on it after I received your instructions. We can expect callbacks, though. The matter was… interesting. I had two appointments with them."

Christian shook his head in amused disbelief. "You wanted to see a dominatrix parlor for once, huh?"

Peter laughed. "No. Cathrine and I believed to have a rudimentary understanding of what they actually wanted. It would have been an exciting challenge."

Christian grinned knowingly. "Sure."

Peter unclasped his hands in a helpless gesture. "Hey, I wanted to try it. In my opinion, the site is about as far from smut as it gets. Your decision is a pity and a bit premature if I may say so."

Christian nodded slowly. "I can understand what you thought so challenging about it, but we don't make sites for such businesses."

Peter repeated his gesture. "You're going to have to cancel the client."

Christian snorted. "I'll moderate it, no problem."

Peter was annoyed by this word. "Moderate" – a prime example from the arrogant vocabulary of an over-the-top business guy. It meant "skillfully letting someone's inquiry fizzle out by stalling and purposeful dalliance until an excuse was found not to deal with it." Peter wondered how Ms. Jana would react to the perfidious not-and-then-again rejection by a man she didn't know. She would surely be disappointed. He smiled to himself. Why didn't he suppose the dominatrix would react angrily? He determinedly raised his head and looked at Christian. Boring ol' SEO-Pete seemed to have changed quite a bit during his vacation; certainly, the result of the unaccustomed responsibility he had been given. "Moderate it, Chris," Peter said with a mild smile.

Janice opened the door without knocking and raised her eyebrows appreciatively when she caught sight of him: well behaved, quiet, and on his knees. She had probably hoped to catch him in the act of something forbidden, or at least to interrupt him in something.

Michael humbly bowed his head. "Lady Janice." Janice wore a long, dark brown dress whose sleeves cast a wide wreath of white ruffles around her wrists. A wide-brimmed, equally brown hat sat at an angle on her head like a beret, and a hawk's gray-and-white mottled feather jutted far from the snow-white hatband. An overly wide leather belt with a silver buckle and well-worn holes trimmed the wide, almost baggy dress to give it a narrow waist. The past few days had made Michael more observant. He began to *read* the ladies. The brown, the hawk feather, the scuffed belt: Janice's outfit was an exaggerated, impractical homage to the garb of an archaic huntsman, like a carnival costume, yet unerringly accurate as a good caricature. The long dress prevented a view of the shaft of her boots, but their tips flashed out beneath.

Janice tilted her head in an unabashedly corrosive smile. "Michael. You were expecting me?"

He nodded humbly. "Yes, Lady Janice. I would not have forgiven myself being in the shower or worse, still asleep, when you arrived."

Janice licked her lips. "Little Cherry snitched, didn't she?"

Fuck. This was going to cost Cherry dearly. But what was he supposed to do? Lie? Only Janice knew who she had told about her appointment today, and apparently the circle of those in question was so small that her first guess was correct already. "Yes, Lady Janice," he said curtly.

The domina grinned broadly. "Good slave."

By the time Peter was back at his own desk, the anticipated email from Ms. Jana had arrived. He cursed quietly; an hour earlier and he could have used the info therein for the conversation with Christian.

Dear Mr. Wartmann,

I would like to thank you for the informative conversation we had last week. Regrettably, you as yet have not sent me a contract to sign, as you announced. My colleagues and I are very much looking forward to the new website and have no intention of letting it be derailed by formalities or circumstances of personal nature.

Perhaps I need to apologize to you? Our enterprise is unusual for certain and neither myself nor my colleagues had thought that working with us might be a burden for people who had only minimal exposure to our lifestyle beforehand. Did you take my advice to heart? I would not forgive myself if interacting with me made you feel uncomfortable.

As announced, I have figured out a way to lay a better conceptual approach for you in the type of person we are trying to target. I invite you very cordially to another joint appointment. You will come today at 2 pm. I look forward to seeing you.

Sincerely yours,

Jana

Peter repeated his silent curse. He really should forward this email to Christian, so that the deputy agency manager could diplomatically decline the assignment. Now Ms. Jana had woven some personal information into her text that he didn't particularly want his superior to know. In addition, there was the ladies' bad habit of setting appointments entirely at their own discretion and insinuating that he constantly had time on his hands and was only waiting for their invitations.

Michael had seen through the routines. At least he thought he had. The ladies of the house would get the slaves they were entrusted with for the day and tutor them. Each slave probably was at a different stage of growth, so the lessons were tailored for each individual guest. So far, each of the ladies had found it necessary to look at him ponderously, touching his body with barely restrained anticipation, sizing him up and examining him. In a way, it had been a mutual introduction. Janice was different. She sat down in a chair by the window, took off her impractical hat, and pointed to his bed. "You found the drawer?"

He shook his head. "Sorry, no, Lady Janice. I don't know what you're talking about."

She snorted. "Turn the wooden decorative knob on the lower right bedpost clockwise."

He was about to rise, but immediately interrupted the potentially disastrous move. A glance in her direction was enough to assure himself of the wisdom of that decision. He crawled toward his bed and turned the wooden knob with the small silver ornamental cap that encompassed its pole like the ornaments of an oriental tower. A soft snap sounded, and one of the ebony trims opened a finger's width. He opened the cleverly hidden secret compartment and had no idea what he was looking at.

Peter would go to Ms. Jana and communicate the refusal to her in person. Her friendly, elegant nature deserved more than an email riddled with half-baked politicking that nullified her charming, as well as challenging, little website. He imagined Ms. Jana, looking up from her laptop in her beautiful dress, utterly disappointed, and having to explain to her colleagues that Mr. Wartmann's boss had prohibited him from working with them any further. He exhaled slowly. He didn't want to disappoint Ms. Jana. She was to have her little website, and she was to have it the way she wanted it. *Maybe*, he thought to himself, *I can build the site in my free time?* A domain can be purchased in no time. The structure is so straightforward; it could be done with one of the many free content management systems.

He loaded his current keyword analysis and continued working on the site of a printshop that had expanded its portfolio to include custom windshield decals. Peter evaluated a few competitors and realized that the poor company didn't stand a chance. At least not with a budget like his. There were three competitors in his area alone who optimized for "custom rear-window decals" as well as "foiling and stickers for cars." He needed another catch.

Janice seized the two narrow wooden strips, connected by two screws, with pointed fingers. "I'm not as scholarly as Selina," she whispered, pinching Michael in the cheek, "But I pride myself in my experience, made in the best studios all over the world. This lovely contraption is made in Germany and bears the very crude name 'Hodenklemme.' How would you translate that, slave?"

Michael swallowed and looked at the object about thirty centimeters long, made of two slender wooden slats lying on top of each other. "Hoe-den-klammy…?" he mumbled fearfully, butchering the pronunciation. "I'm afraid I have no idea, Lady Janice."

Janice pursed her lips. "You'll have an idea soon." She gathered her dress and stretched out a leg. Her walnut brown boots were knee high and laced in a beautiful, intricate pattern. Michael saw a small, metal object flash between the laces, tucked in there on purpose. "The key to your penis cage, slave. Get hold of it." Michael's hands slid hesitantly toward the imperiously placed boot in front of him. Janice's hands hesitated far less and gave him a resounding slap. "With your mouth, moron."

Dear Ms. Jana,

Thank you for your email. You are correct: I have not sent you a contract yet. Please await our meeting this afternoon, which I will be happy to confirm, regarding this formality. I am looking forward to seeing you later, as well as to our further appointment.

As for your other question, yes, I took your advice to heart and told my girlfriend about the venture. She didn't take it well and temporarily moved into a friend's house. She refers to it as a "pause" in the relationship. Well, "He gave me a piece of his mind, and I snapped like a mousetrap" is probably just not going to accommodate Luisa's ego :-) You were right in many things, Ms. Jana.

This private matter shall not prevent me from continuing to work alongside the ladies of the house. See you this afternoon.

Yours sincerely,

Peter Wartmann

He clicked send and cleared his throat in relief.

Sandra glanced around her screen. "Something wrong?"

He shook his head. "No, everything's okay. I'll be off this afternoon though, from 1 pm. Private thing."

Sandra turned back to her work. "No prob for me. Have you seen my analysis for the medieval mill?"

Michael bent down to Janice's boot and tried to push the tightly tied laces apart with his lips, enough for his teeth to bite the key. The small shiny piece of metal had been placed with guile, so he had to toss his head around at Janice's feet to uncover it bit by bit.

"You are only here half a year, slave," she taunted him for his slowness.

He mumbled an "Excuse me, Lady Janice" and managed to free the round head of the key. He almost strained his neck, but finally bit into the metal and sighed with relief.

She snorted in discontent. "Great, I only grew ten gray hairs in the meantime. Open your chastity device." Michael obeyed and placed the pink cage on the floor beside him.

Janice nodded toward the bed. "Turn over. One hand on each knob of the bedpost, standing upright." Again he obeyed, touching the cool metal on the two wooden balls that finished his bedposts. Behind him, he heard a light switch ping, followed by the rustle of a bunch of keys and a soft squeak, as if a small chest were being opened. Janice's heels came closer. "The metal in the bedposts works a lot like the heart rate monitors on gym machines. As long as your hands stay on them – and a heartbeat registers – you're fine. However, if you let go of either one…"

Out of nowhere, a vicious blow hit him on the back of his thighs that could only have come from a riding whip or a similar slender, jerking instrument. Michael cried out abruptly and let go of the right bedpost to touch the stricken spot. An electric shock ran through the left side of his body, where his hand still remained on the bedpost. A second, no less surprised scream erupted from his throat.

"Got it?" Janice asked coldly.

Michael nodded, his face contorted with pain, and put

both hands back on the metal. "Yes, Lady Janice."

A visibly cheerful Ms. Jana was waiting for Peter in the driveway. She wore a wide, flowing, folded skirt and pretty, bright-heeled shoes. Her hair curled, and again not curled in such a remarkable way, lay open on her shoulders. A blouse matching the summery skirt, but more stringently cut, prevented the outfit from being girly. Peter shook her hand and again she leaned forward for two sweet, breathy kisses on his cheeks.

"Today," she promised, knowingly raising a finger, "We're going to make progress, Mr. Wartmann. I've invited someone to join our conversation who will help with our research for your important keyword."

Peter grinned. "That would be great. However, I would be happy if we could talk for a few minutes, Ms. Jana. There…" – he sighed – "there's a problem."

She raised her brows. "Oh, I'd love to. Does it have to do with your girlfriend? I was" – she paused for a moment – "a little conflicted about your email this morning. How do you feel?"

Peter waved it off. "That' s another story. I want to talk to you about the project. My boss is against the site."

Jana instantly understood what he meant. "Then why did he let you work on it for two weeks?"

Peter smiled thinly. "He was on vacation. I'm his second-in-command and simply accepted the assignment out of… fascination. He returned in the meantime and made it clear that, unfortunately, he does not want to accept the gig. I told him that I would have liked to do the site and continue to work on it."

Jana nodded quietly. "I'm not familiar with the ways of doing business in your industry," she said softly. "But why didn't you put that in the email and why did you come here anyway?"

Peter cleared his throat. "Because I'd like to do the site," he repeated, a hopeful smile sliding across his face.

"As mentioned, I have neither the education of Lady Selina," Janice continued behind him, the slender whipping instrument traveling along his thigh, patting his exposed privates with draconian caresses, "nor the athleticism of Tatjana or the majesty of Jana. Whether I even want to possess the nymphomania of Carlotta is debatable. However, I also don't define myself by the things I possess or control" – she bent over his back as if taking him doggy style and whispered in his ear – "but rather by what I don't possess: patience, grace, consideration." She laughed throatily and took a step back again. A shadow on the wall above his pillow revealed her arm reaching out to strike a low blow. "Do my lack of mercy a favor and make this loud, slave."

The first blow drove into the back of his knee. Michael cried out in dismay and was about to collapse but held on to the bedposts. Already a film of cold sweat was forming in his palms. Janice chuckled softly. "Count, idiot." The second blow whipped his tense shin muscles and burned like fire. Michael's brain was bombarded by countless emotions and sensory input, but he managed to get something right again and counted the second lash between clenched teeth as "one."

Janice hummed as amazed as she was pleased. "We're up to speed, aren't we?"

Michael produced a growled, "Yes, Lady Janice."

She raised the whip again. "Good boy." The third stroke drew a vicious red line across his buttocks. He winced and his cock dangled, quivering between his thighs. Janice giggled. "Oh, slave. You're not at all used to it! What did your Lady Elaine do to you? Drip hot wax on your little belly? Dildo play but no sticking in? Handcuffs on the bedpost and other couples' shit that only passes for sadomasochism with a lot of good will?" She grabbed his hair and jerked his head back. "When I'm done with you, you're going to beg your dear Elaine to rape you with a strap-on." Michael whimpered painfully as Janice threatened to pull out a tuft of his hair. The dominatrix laughed. "She will flourish, thanks to you."

The pain became more intense the longer the castigation lasted, as more and more frequently Janice hit spots that were already reddened. "In the old days," she crooned during a small pause, "We called this a warm-up. Today, it's part of the game. The young slaves have become self-centered if you ask me. In a cotton candy world that hands out medals for participation and where the mileage of my neighbor's sports car is the biggest problem of my jealous little existence, it's a real sensation to get spanked." A soft thump sounded, and she let him know by means of a gentler tap on the underside of his upper arms that the power was off. He disengaged his trembling hands from the bedposts and sank to his knees, hissing in pain.

Janice looked down at him. "You have the potential to be a good man. A lamb to the lady, a wolf to the world." She stroked his chest with the tip of the riding whip. "I used to tame, now I parent," she hissed in disgust and spat in Michael's face.

Jana opened her mouth, closed it again, and reopened it.

Peter ducked guiltily. "Only if you want me to."

She blinked twice in confusion, and Peter involuntarily wondered if anyone had ever made a dominatrix react like that. After an awkward moment of surprised silence, they both laughed abruptly.

"Well," Jana finally articulated, covering a rasp of her throat with a majestic gesture, "Don't you need any special programs for that? I'm afraid our IT is limited to the most economically necessary, as far as managing a quasi-hotel is concerned."

He shrugged. "It's all on my laptop." He tapped against his bag. "What I do with it after hours is my business." He sighed. "Ms. Jana, I don't want to be intrusive. You were right to turn to an agency that can – in theory – take care of the whole package of analysis, design, setup, go-live, management, and maintenance for you. I was the idiot and didn't even pitch the task to my team for consideration."

She tilted her head. "So, you can do the site on your own?"

He nodded. "Yes. We might even be a little freer in terms of styling that way. We'll do an analysis and come up with a great design. Do you have pictures of the estate? Because that would be great for the wide graphic envisioned. Preferably with the little lake and driveway in it. Then we do the text, which has to really hit home with the reader. Then, if something changes and the site needs to be taken down quickly – I have no idea what might happen in your industry – I'll do it with one click. From anywhere. And we cou—"

She stepped up beside him with a sweeping motion, interrupting his torrent of excited words therewith. Her skirt fluttered in a whisper, and she clasped her hand to his, smiling broadly. "We'll make a great site, Mr. Wartmann?"

He smiled in surprise. "Um. Yes?"

Ms. Jana took a first step beneath the portal displaying the Medusa. "That sounds just wonderful."

"It' s almost uncomfortable to be asked about it so directly," the handsome man in the snow-white shirt admitted, crossing his arms with a smile. Peter had hiccupped at the sight of him. The man was a single act of genetic bravado, the sheer sight of which caused a sense of inadequacy in anyone who looked at him. His face seemed carved from warm, living stone. His dark, slightly curly hair possessed the endearing sass that makes Mediterraneans so attractive to many women, and his every gesture spoke of the calculated restraint of a genius who could silence anyone present with a single remark, yet was too benevolent to do so. He was – as far as Peter could make such an assessment of another man – an incredible beauty.

Tobias Roudette, Fourteen, was a manufactured product of the house. And he was… perfect. White teeth shone from a subtly tanned face, and muscles stretched beneath the white shirt, giving him such a frustratingly enviable, decently broad-shouldered silhouette that Peter unconsciously adjusted his posture in his seat. Fourteen, Ms. Jana assured him, had been asked not to behave as usual in the house, but to help them determine keywords at absolute eye level. When Peter had asked what had drawn him to Ms. Jana's house, he had leaned back, a little embarrassed. "There was, I can tell you that much, no single moment of realization. Rather, it was a constellation of situations and occurrences that led me here. Sexual frustration wasn't as big a factor as you'd think," he explained in answer to Peter's agape mouth, leaving an impressed analyst wondering how Fourteen could have known he was going to be asked about this.

The product grinned softly and Peter involuntarily replied with a grin of his own. "I've always had a penchant for a certain sexual practice that – forgive me – I'd rather not explain in front of someone I've never met before. Don't worry, it's as legal as it is unspectacular. I just value my privacy."

Peter nodded understandingly.

Fourteen glanced at Jana. "It drove me, although I had a record of success with women, to the studio of a dominatrix named Lady Caroline at irregular intervals. Her pseudonym was Mistress Cara van Rouge. The amorous relationship with her was a constant in my life. One of the few. I realized that I valued trips to her more than success in a job that bored me or the judgment of partners I could replace at will. I kept Caroline a secret from those partners, of course. I didn't want to hurt anyone. One day" – he laughed silently, raising his arms in an apologetic gesture –

"What a platitude! *One day*, the number of straining fragments, constantly threatening to break further, in which my life unfolded, seemed to have gone over my head. I," he huffed, "I-I wanted love, yet had relationships. I wanted a profession, yet had a job. As I mentioned, there was no single moment when I became aware that I was not living the life of a normal person but was putting on a show that merely mimicked a normal life as best I could. There was only a kind of slow understanding that something was going completely wrong here."

"The fact that I have to administer parenting to men that their parents have failed to do is scandalous in itself. This… *fixation* on the cock just kills it," Janice grumbled, and Michael received a slap of frustration, which he took vicariously for all modern men. Into his pained groans rattled the wooden slats of the strange device with the unpronounceable name. "In the old days, the fetishistic act was sensation," Janice whispered, looking ruefully at the mysterious toy. "To kneel, to rule, to play, to switch roles, and to have coffee together afterwards, heads bright red, bringing each other back down to earth with sexually loaded snickering. Woman and man" – she clacked the wooden slats like castanets – "were allies. Now we're clients and providers." Her gaze turned ice cold. "And you have been paid for, slave. Stand up, turn around, and slide your sack between your thighs like a little boy playing girl."

He did as she commanded but found this position more than odd. She looked down at his bare butt, his balls protruding underneath like an animal's. Janice snorted. "Oh, you're going to love this, slave." She gripped his testicles with ice-cold fingers. Michael gave a startled groan. The wooden strips settled over and under his testicles, and Janice closed the two threads with quick twists of her fingers. "Looks a bit like somebody put two bald men in one of those medieval public humiliation devices for people to throw stuff at them in humi—" – she snapped her fingers – "Humbler! That's an adequate translation."

Michael drew air through his teeth with pain. The device clamped his testicles to the back, the wooden bars sitting right in the crease between his buttocks and thighs. If he tried to straighten his upper body, he would run a serious risk of hurting himself in a terrible way. At the same time, his balls were "defenseless," purred Janice, giving him the worst foot stomp he had ever felt. The reflex to jerk himself upright immediately triggered a second wave of pain. The humbler forced him onto all fours; he couldn't even sit down without squeezing his testicles. So Michael whined and hissed, degradingly trying to find the least painful position at Janice's feet.

"You'd be surprised at the stretchiness of male scrotal skin," Janice commented in the manner of a voiceover in an animal documentary. "I have a private slave who is no longer in pain at all." Michael sniffled, and she rolled her eyes, "God, you're pathetic. A minimum of fighting spirit please." She kicked his exposed, defenseless balls again with the toe of her boot. Michael screamed in a mixture of razor-sharp pain and growing frustration at his defenselessness.

"In a period of extreme depression, I confessed these thoughts to Lady Caroline. She understood me and asked if I would be willing to undergo a complete change in my life in order to be happy. Every day, I faced evidence of my capabilities, whose constant underuse almost drove me mad. So I said yes. She promised to bring a friend to our next get-together, someone who might be able to help me."

Peter looked over at the lovingly smiling Ms. Jana, who nodded in affirmation.

Fourteen sighed. "It took courage to make this decision. I'll admit that in all honesty. But I am absolutely convinced that I have done the right thing."

Peter took a deep breath. "Why did this drastic change seem to make the most sense to you? Sorry – don't get me wrong – but a boring job can be quit, and the right partner can be found."

Fourteen smiled. "Right. However, I think I would have been bored in any job and no conventionally findable partner would have made me happy." At this statement, he coyly rubbed his hands together in his lap, "God, that sounds incredibly narcissistic."

Ms. Jana shook her head. Peter was silent on the matter, but he agreed with the perfect man on this.

"The most appropriate comparison for my feelings," Fourteen said, "would be with a painter who lives for his poor-selling art and therefore makes a living creating advertising posters. Even though I'm not an artist. I feel" – he smiled disarmingly – "that I've risen from being a *bystander* of life to a *participant* in it. My experiences here are my own."

Janice proved that she didn't need a sophisticated studio full of equipment and toys. The domina of the house was able to create maximum pain with minimal effort. She had put a dog leash on Michael and walked the whimpering slave. The humbler on Michael's private parts made crawling on all fours a challenge: a leg stretched too far back pulled on the wooden toy, sending agonizing aches through his martyred abdomen. He was forced to limp like a wounded animal, making small leaps and clumsy steps. Janice greeted the oncoming ladies effusively and bursts of laughter erupted from the open doors they passed. Naked female slaves gathered into trembling, anxiously whispering clusters in the corners and doorways. Male slaves widened their eyes in fright at the sight of Michael and hurried to look even busier than they already were. Janice led him to a staircase and watched patiently as he shakily made his way down. Arms ahead, legs trailing slowly, watching for any movement.

"One actually does become humble, doesn't he?" she asked, and he fretted at being pulled from his fear-fueled concentration.

"Yes, Lady Janice," he said, taking another step. The dominatrix strode behind at a measured pace. Without having the muse or the time to look up at her, the image of the Huntress and her loyal dog coalesced in his mind.

Fourteen leaned forward. There was real helpfulness and honest concern about the benefits of his contribution in his beautiful eyes. "Does this help you? Can you get anything… out of this?"

Peter took a slow breath and cleared his throat. "I think so, though I need to process all that I've heard first. Anyway, I have to express my gratitude to you. You did a great job of putting the feelings into words."

Fourteen raised his handsome head with an amused grin, and Ms. Jana suppressed a charming snicker.

Peter wondered for a moment what was so funny, until his own little betrayal occurred to him. He cleared his throat again. "Hrm! Meaning, I can now better imagine you as a resident of the hou—uh, I can now relate super well to a person with this sexuali—"

Ms. Jana laughed out loud, and Fourteen put his hand in front of his mouth in amusement.

"It's okay, Mr. Wartmann," she said, putting her hand on his arm.

Peter snorted and joined them in their laughter.

"Actually, we committed a little crime, slave," Janice purred as they strode down a hallway filled with paintings and wonderful plasterwork. Michael looked up warily. He didn't even trust his neck muscles anymore, after just about every fiber of his body emitted some painful impulse from the humbler. Every movement of his hips and back required thoughtful consideration, not to mention his legs.

"How did we commit this crime, Lady Janice?"

The lady let the chain rattle softly. "Lady Jana has a guest. She does not wish us to show ourselves in the corridors. At least not in this *getup*," she said, pointing to Michael's protruding balls. "You're not quite pleasing to the eye, my lanky little thrift store hunk. And that sore shade of red doesn't suit your sack."

Michael politely asked forgiveness for his fashion faux pas and followed Janice to the front of a grand door. "I've invited guests to tea myself, slave," she informed him with her hand on the handle. "They are young ladies who hope to secure a permanent place in the house." She paused for a moment, and Michael thought she was once again reminiscing. Janice smiled thinly, and he sensed that she seemed to have accepted him in her own way.

She said nothing for an uncomfortably long moment, and he dared to ask quietly, "…Lady Janice?"

She looked down at him. "Some of those clucking chickens who call themselves dominatrixes these days should be groveling in your place, slave. Let's just leave it at that." She pushed the handle down, then paused again. "Which doesn't mean you should disobey them. I do have a reputation to lose."

As the three participants of the conversation settled down again, a relaxed atmosphere of fraternization reverberated in Ms. Jana's office. Peter's cheeks were flushed, and Fourteen displayed the cultivated amusement of a theater critic who believed he had detected an homage to an old maestro in an avant-garde play. Even if Ms. Jana had still had any doubts about the trigger of Mr. Wartmann's fascination, they were now gone.

"It's no secret," Fourteen said slowly, "that people with this kind of sexuality often ask themselves questions. Especially in adolescence. Starting with those about the pleasure of affectionate pain to actual philosophy, which always sounds terribly erratic coming from the mouths of laymen like me. I delight in the role of a Shaolin student."

He laughed again, and Ms. Jana blew out in ironic amazement. "Oho!" Fourteen raised a hand. "By that, I mean this whole procedure of practice, asceticism, and subsequent reward to asceticism and practice. I am good at kneeling. I've been working on that for a long time. The woman I want to kneel before should be worth it." Jana smiled wider than before.

Peter nodded slowly. "So," he rhetorically asked, "You have internalized asceticism and mastered the exercises?"

Tobias Roudette opened his hands. "Most decidedly, yes. Only Nirvana has not yet arrived to bid for me."

Jana tilted her head in a loving smile. "It will soon, honey. I promise."

The room Janice led Michael into was a light-filled lounge. A white and gold table with a glass top stood in its center, surrounded by wide seating with round, exuberantly flowing backrests. Bookshelves lined the walls. Side tables placed by the doors and next to the seating revealed that relaxed afternoons of tea ceremonies, card games, and other social activities could be spent here. Four young women rose from the bulky seating and respectfully greeted Janice. One by one, each lady introduced herself: Laura, Jessica, Theresa, and Desirae. Theresa and Jessica even gave a very formal curtsy, which elicited a smirk from Janice.

"I am delighted to host four such beautiful ladies in the house," Janice said. "And I would like to ask you right at the very beginning not to tackle our conversation with the deathly earnestness of a job interview. As you can see, I haven't made any particular effort in choosing my company either." She pointed to Michael. The four young women laughed raucously.

"I was about to ask if the infamous house had to lower its standards that much," the blonde woman named Laura said, crudely grabbing Michael's chin so she could look at him.

Janice giggled. "Not at all, dear Laura. Rather, this little slave is my project for today. I am not a theoretician, but a practitioner. And that, ladies, is the practice that I – and with a little luck, you soon – will be working on: puny, downright underdeveloped, limp, and repulsive at first glance."

Theresa purred amusedly, "And that was just the description of his penis."

"Resilience," Peter said, looking into Ms. Jana's face as she returned from the door where she had seen Fourteen off.

Jana tilted her head. "Resilience?"

Peter nodded. "The principle of mental defensibility. Sorry, that sounds pretentious. But I think we've found the root of the matter. We just need to break it down a little. Make it a no-brainer that immediately switches a flick in our viewers' minds."

Jana sat back down and looked at Peter in surprise. "Do explain to me how you came up with that word?"

He opened his laptop. "I picked up three important terms in Fourteen's story. Or rather, there was not the one moment – as he correctly pointed out – but three factors at once, the meaning of which does not seem to be entirely clear to him, that led Tobias Roudette to your house. He *understood* his problem in a certain way." Peter enumerated on the first finger: "He felt more than capable of tackling it" – he touched a second finger – "but was faced with the problem of implementation, or *do-ability*, the big *how. How* was he going to change his life, which he associated with infuriating boredom, disappointment, and constant unfulfillment? End another relationship, change jobs, see Lady Caroline more often, who was threatening to become his sole remaining source of joy? The house, Ms. Jana" – Peter touched a third finger – "the house itself has shown him a way to solve his problem. Even if he had already mastered all…" – he gestured and Jana smiled warmly at the analyst talking himself into a frenzy – "all, um, the practices and had been a ladies' man before, he lacked the idea of the *attainability* of his goal called 'happiness.' Although, admittedly, it must be rare to speak of being bought by a wealthy woman as a lofty goal in life – no offense intended."

Jana just smiled silently. A ruddering gesture prompted Peter to continue. She would not make the mistake of halting his delightful flux of words.

Peter leaned forward, and Jana felt an excited tingle crawl up and down her spine. "The main keyword, Ms. Jana" – his smile became triumphant – "has to do with feasibility and achievability. Purposefulness, in other words, 'Why do I want this?' And *understandability* of the problem has to be present in order to even run into the problem called 'And how do I solve this?'"

To this point, Michael had absorbed the lessons of the ladies of the house like a sponge. There were dynamics in this form of sexuality that he could not put into words, but he could feel them, anticipate them, grow from them, or falter at them. There was no end to the game, only crossroads leading in new directions. He sensed the trap before it snapped shut and tilted his torso to the floor, where his head paused inches above the ladies' feet.

"Are you going to greet the ladies, slave?" Janice asked, and he literally heard her surprised, yet delighted smile. Janice would have reminded him in a few seconds via slap, or worse, of the duty to greet mistresses in a manner befitting their status.

Call me puny one more time, he thought, pursing his lips to lower them gratefully to Laura's toes. The ladies were festively dressed. The young woman gathered her dark blue skirt to give Michael's lips full access to her feet, which were in black high heels. She had soft, warm toes that smelled wonderful. Where the skin slowly became sole, a telltale, lovely redness of a woman perpetually standing in high heels shone. Michael sighed softly and touched the almost hot skin longingly with his lips. Laura was indeed nervous and had been sweating a little. This appointment was of great importance. Her pedicure received several affectionate kisses until she pushed his head along with a rough, almost the force of a kick, wipe of her other foot. "Don't forget the other mistresses, scumbag," she snarled.

Jana nodded slowly as she repeated Peter's words in her head. "It's about feasibility of…?" she asked skeptically.

Peter raised his hands. "The feasibility of happiness. We are bridging the gap to my original thought about happiness of life. It wasn't wrong but just had a much too lofty, romantic altitude of thought. The raw material of your products" – he rose – "as you know yourself, is made up of men who are looking for something very specific. You used the term 'non-failed existences.' We should remember that one too, by the way. It's good for copytext. What I want to say is, these men can do anything. They're smart" – he was now pacing excitedly, and Jana's heart was pounding faster with each of his sentences – "They're successful but frustrated, whether it's because of sexuality or the invisible walls they perceive everywhere. Another good expression! Have you worked in marketing before? because you're really good with those! Anyway. We have the following mental prerequisites" – he touched his head almost meditatively and described the funnel he had in mind – "I, as a candidate who doesn't know anything about his luck yet, have gone through the hundredth crisis. I realize I want something different from life. Changes are not difficult for me, I am a go-getter. The world around me is not as great as I am, I am bored in the worst way. To me, life is a dull path whose intersections are sensationalized by every lame duck around me. Being smart, however, I recognize the grim repetition of the same bland rituals in everybody's wedding, in every scandalous dismissal in the boardroom above me, in every new day I have to feel oh-so-special just because today the cloud cover looks different from yesterday. How – and that's where we get involved – do I solve this? I'm not satisfied with a platitude like the good ol' fresh breeze. Should I emigrate? Maybe I just need the right woman?"

Jana smiled at the "we" he didn't even realize he had used. Peter, on the other hand, smiled with pride. "I am capable of too much. I am too free. I am a predator to whom no prey is worthy."

She finished the sentence, "So I crave chains."

After Michael had extensively welcomed three of the ladies into the house – only the woman named Desirae gruffly refused him the honor – they sat down. Janice reined Michael in, and he curled into an almost fetal position at her feet to minimize the pain from the humbler. She placed a boot on his hip and opened her hands. "Ladies, which of you have been guests in Ms. Jana's house before?"

A voice Michael attributed to the woman named Jessica replied, "Once, Lady Janice. A year ago, with a slave. We had booked the apartment with the view of the city."

Janice hummed appreciatively, "A vacation, my dear?"

Jessica nodded eagerly. "Yes, you might say that. I was absolutely fascinated and knew immediately that I wanted to *come* again."

A silly giggle rang out, and Janice's boot quivered softly on Michael's skin. "Who would we be not to appreciate ambiguity?"

The young women laughed louder than the banal joke deserved, and Michael felt an uncomfortable tingle of external shame in his gut. *Sycophants.*

"How did the other three get the idea to apply to us?" Janice asked the group.

The pretty, black-haired Theresa cleared her throat. "A loyal customer brought the house to my attention. He was convinced I possessed some sort of authority to sign people up for a stay here and was disappointed when I had to deny it. Through several lady friends, I finally ran into Barbara Luriel, who told me more about the house."

Janice nodded. "Lady Barbara was present at the auction of a quite excellent vintage two years ago. An impressive young woman – and consequential."

Theresa nodded with a grin. "I treasure my meetings with Barbara, even though I educate less physically than she does. I applied because I believe I am ready to take another step in my development. And this is where I'm being offered a most unique opportunity to do so."

"Sometimes freedom calls for chains," Peter intoned, spreading his arms as if the words were written on the wall in neon letters.

Jana leaned back with a grin and crossed her legs. "Our headline?"

Peter cradled his head on his shoulders. "The headline should contain the final keyword. It's more like our motto, the theme that runs through the page."

Jana nodded, impressed. "I like it."

He sat back down and placed the notebook in his lap. "So, let's recapitulate: feasibility, meaning, understanding. Freedom, boredom, escape, life goals, happiness. All terms we need."

Jana understood. "Is it better to address the men directly?"

Peter nodded, typing. "I recommend that, yes. Better than having the site just sound informative."

She frowned. "What's more important? Repeating the ultimate keyword multiple times or covering a lot of words that go in the right direction?"

Peter hummed, impressed, "Good question, Ms. Jana. The final keyword is important to have in the URL as well as in the big headline. Elsewhere, synonyms, explanatory phrases, and context may be used. The days of stuffing web pages with the same word are over."

After the somewhat overzealous Laura had also delivered a veritable sexual revival story, of course remembering to praise the house beyond measure, Janice turned to Desirae. "And you, my dear?"

Lady Desirae pursed a corner of her mouth and eyed those present, including the quietly repose Michael, with a piqued, almost embarrassed look. She had refused Michael's greeting with an indignant "Eww, naw… Fuck off, ya' disgustin'." Dermal anchor piercings shone like twin tears on her tanned cheekbones. An accurately trimmed fringe fell to just above her eyelids. "I'm Lady Dee Delanox. I have seventy-one thousand followers on social media, and nine hundred on Pay-Slavery dot com. Twenty of them are subscribed to Findom-Queensize and send me $300 bucks monthly. The rest pay $5 a month for the Pay-Piggie membership. I'm here because one of my main pay pigs told me to check it out. I might have wanted to do a few posts about it, because the interior is like, so cool, but you can screw that. The muscly naked guy with the little blonde bitch took my cell phone away, like at the entrance of some fancy-ass brothel."

Silence ensued.

Janice exchanged one boot on Michael's hip for the other. "That's a… response," she breathed, and Michael literally heard the diabolical grin on her face. "A highly interesting one at that. Explain to me how you might defend against a shift in the dominant-devotee dynamic, when surely it's your subscribers' demands and their related willingness to pay that determines the nature and ultimate shape of your content?"

Michael almost laughed out loud.

Lady Dee Delanox bubbled. "Huh?"

Janice cooed sweetly. "Excuse me, my dear. I've been very cryptic. Here's a new one: Darling, are you a dominatrix, or can any fool with a PayPal account order high-resolution pictures of your asshole stretched to the max?"

"Discovering oneself," Jana pitched to Peter.

The latter shook his head skeptically. "A little too much on the *Eat Pray Love* side."

She snorted. "Breaking out." He wasn't satisfied with that either and again began pacing up and down her office, both so Victorian and so ultra-modern. Jana crossed her legs and watched her web specialist. He had blanked out the world. She smiled softly and, having run out of ideas, opened her laptop to find a website for synonyms and clever quotes that might help her. Peter mutteringly rejected the "personal growth," "advancement," and "goal achievement" suggestions that came from there. Then his heels came to a quiet thumping halt, and he looked over at Jana.

After Lady Dee Delanox left them with her red head spinning, Janice turned her attention to the remaining three ladies. "I care nothing for the humiliation of other women," she explained, "But I do care for the atmosphere in my employer's house and for a balance of heterogeneous minds pursuing the same goal. I am the Domina." The three young ladies nodded in unison. "And you are my frontrunners for the advertised position. Mistress Isabella has left the establishment, the master student of dear Lady Selina, who takes care of cultural instruction and etiquette. The three of you have academic degrees?" Unanimous nods. Janice snorted. "You are welcome to speak. No need for false shyness." Her boot lifted from Michael's hip, and she placed it on his head. "I'm no cannibal after all."

Jana looked into the flushed face of Peter Wartmann. "The better life," the analyst breathed and opened his hands in a gesture hoping for evaluation as well as approval. Jana siphoned the extremely simple words through the filter of concepts that had formed in her head during the last four hours. At the end of her deliberation was a wolfish grin. Her eyes, the color of dark honey, shone, framed by her out-of-this-world mane of brunette hair, as she rose and approached him with measured steps, heels clicking softly.

Peter Wartmann was the right man for the job.

CHAPTER 6: SONATA OF THE NIGHT

"The ladies of the house feel like celebrating," Cherry whispered, tapping against Michael's thigh. He cleared his throat awkwardly and spread his legs as her mechanical, trained touch had demanded. Cherry stirred thoughtfully in a small jar. Michael watched her intently. Her little silver spoon kept bumping against the porcelain, and she peered into the opening with an odd, disconcerting curiosity. "I haven't been around long enough to have witnessed one, but I think there's going to be an auction soon. It may also have something to do with the stranger who visits so frequently at Ms. Jana's. Who knows?"

Michael repeated his throat clearing. "And what does that have to do with you and me?"

Cherry was a little older than Michael and looked at him lovingly from her snow-white face. "I have no idea," she said, lifting the small porcelain jar, "But I'm supposed to rub this ointment on you. Don't worry, it smells like an ordinary skin lotion. Lady Derya mixed food coloring into it and instructed me to stir it constantly."

Cherry escorted Michael to the front of one of the large salons on the second floor. The muffled voices of the mistresses could be heard. "Do you know," he asked quietly, looking nervously and, at the same time, perplexedly down his naked body, "What they're gonna do to me?"

Cherry looked at him, no less puzzled. The lotion she had been rubbing on him had left a golden film on his skin. "You," Cherry whispered, holding her hand over her mouth in amusement, "look like a life-size Oscar award."

Michael snorted. "Great." The curvy little slave girl was right, though; he did look like a golden statue. Cherry had even applied it to his penis after having freed it from its humiliating cage, which elicited a sigh of relief from Michael.

"Suits you," she whispered, almost poking him in the side in a buddy-like fashion but holding back so as not to smear the paint.

Michael shook his head. "And now?"

"Now," Lady Selina's voice hummed from behind the two naked slaves, "It's time to celebrate, my pretties." Michael and Cherry wheeled around. The slave immediately went to her knees, and Michael would have done the same if a raised index finger from Selina hadn't halted him. "We don't want to ruin the carpet." He nodded significantly. Selina wore a strapless, tight-fitting cocktail dress of a blue so dark it seemed almost black. Her feet were in open-toed high heels whose two thin leather straps shone in the same blue-black. One held the shoes at the ankle, the other curled over the base of her immaculate, straight toes. Michael sighed, lustful at her view. A subtle, lovely pedicure kept all attention focused on the sleek, elegant shoes and the shape of her pretty feet, rather than dragging it to the toes. Cherry knelt and Selina extended her left foot forward. The slave's lips lowered to her toes and gave each one a long, intense kiss. Michael bit his lip in envy. How he would have loved to trade places with Cherry.

"That'll do, honey," Selina said, withdrawing her foot from Cherry. The slave straightened her upper body and placed her hands in her lap obediently. Lady Selina looked at Michael and pointed to the door. "We're going to enter. You sit on the fur by the fireplace and be quiet, Cherry. Michael, you will find a stool covered with plastic wrap in front of the window. Kneel on it."

The salon was full of mistresses. When Selina, Cherry, and Michael entered, a few heads turned toward them, but most were engrossed in relaxed conversation or helping themselves at a buffet. Champagne glasses clinked, and individual bursts of laughter flared up again and again among the small groups. In a central seating area, Ms. Jana, Janice, Derya, and Carlotta were lounging. Tatjana was talking to two other mistresses at the window. Michael believed all of the fully trained ladies of the house were here. He had picked up the number of seventeen actual mistresses somewhere in conversation with other slaves on his floor but couldn't recount in the professional hurry he made toward the quickly found plastic-wrapped stool.

"Oho," Janice said aloud, "Look at this shining man of ours here!" Michael had knelt on the generous stool, an antique ottoman, rustling loudly with the plastic wrap that protected the fabric from the gold paint on his skin. Now, almost all the mistresses of the house turned, and an astonished murmur rose.

"That looks awesome, Seli," Carlotta giggled.

Lady Selina winked. "You'll be thrilled, my dears. But please bear with me for a few moments. I have to prepare him."

Most of the ladies resumed their conversations, but Derya, Tatjana, and two other mistresses approached with interest. Lady Derya, the curvy maîtresse de cuisine, raised a hand and had a hard time restraining herself from curiously running it over Michael's skin. "This turned out better than I thought," she rejoiced. "I tried it years ago with pink, on a slave girl. Looked more like Miss Piggy, though."

The women laughed while Michael looked anxiously at an object made of countless thin threads and an iron rod that Selina had retrieved from a chest behind them.

"Compliments to little Cherry," said one of the unknown ladies. "She spread it evenly."

Tatjana nodded. "How does it feel, slave? Itchy?"

Michael took his eyes off the object in Selina's hands, which looked like a torture device of the worst kind, and its countless thin cables and ropes that she was arranging.

"No, Lady Tatjana. It feels like a very thick layer of sunscreen."

The ladies nodded. "Very fine. You're glowing like the sun as well, I dare say."

"Now, my dears," Selina fluted, "You'll have to make room for me." The ladies stepped aside and watched eagerly to see what would happen. Michael's heart was pounding. His confusion was complete when Selina placed in his hands what at first glance had looked like the torn handlebars of an antique bicycle: a simple metal bar, a handle on each end. From the bar, between the two handles, fell a myriad of thin wires, almost… Michael raised his eyes in confusion… like the threads of a kite. All the threads converged in a small, oval piece of wood.

"Have I succeeded, or have I succeeded?" asked one of the unknown mistresses at Selina's back.

The concentrating lady nodded softly. "This is your masterpiece, Jeanette. And I want to create my own masterpiece on it. Michael," she said sternly.

He held the strange thing in front of him with justified suspicion. "Yes, Lady Selina?"

She looked down at him. "Raise the bar above your head as far as you can."

He obeyed. The threads, thinning from left to right, slid past his face until the small piece of wood where they all converged hung right in front of his nose. He noticed a small groove in the round wood that he couldn't explain.

"Bite into it," Selina demanded, sounding quite excited. He took a deep breath, stretched his neck, and bit into the piece of wood. His teeth caught the small groove so he could hold it comfortably. What had happened here? He knelt on the stool, his arms stretched far up. At least 40 threads, thinning from left to right, poured from the polished bar toward the piece of wood in his mouth.

"Stay like that," Selina purred.

A tall seat was brought, and Selina's face emerged directly above his as she sat down. The strings cut her sight into narrow strips, but he could clearly see her eyes, shining with excitement. Conversation in the salon had fallen silent. Michael felt the prying eyes of more than a dozen predators on his naked, gilded body, and his submissiveness promptly responded with a sense of welcome surrender and consequent arousal. He did not know what was happening, but he understood that he was being put on display.

Lady Selina winked. "Don't tremble. Don't lower your arms." He nodded gently. She smiled diabolically. "Straighten your back and try to stick your belly out. Even though you are very lanky, little Michael, today you'll be what they call a resonating body." Her slender fingers slid into the threads.

No.

Michael groaned as the realization seeped into his nervous, aroused brain. Those weren't threads. They were *strings.*

Selina turned away for a moment, a soft throbbing sounded. A few of the ladies chuckled in amusement. Then something touched Michael's cock hovering just above the foil on the ottoman chair he was kneeling on. Selina's hands appeared on the strings. It must've been – he almost lowered his head in awesome curiosity – one of her bare feet, touching his thickly lubricated, gold-plated cock. He sighed audibly and closed his eyes in sweet frustration at the sensation of his martyred nerve endings, longing for release since what had felt like an eternity. If they heard his happy sigh, he didn't care now. At that very moment, Selina pulled on one of the strings.

The result of the string's soft vibrations and Michael's involuntary sigh was a sound so touching and ominous, resonating from deep within him, that he shuddered. A few of the ladies let out a soft "Whoa" or an astonished intake of breath. Sugar-sweet sorrow poured into a tone so wistful that even Selina paused for a moment. Michael looked into her eyes through the strings. She looked down at him. It was not necessary, but he nodded. She closed her eyes, and her bare foot slid gently over his shaft. The touch triggered a grateful hum inside him, which, over two more delicate plucks, turned into sounds. Biting the little piece of wood, he felt the vibration of the strings in his jaw. Selina's toes reached Michael's moist tip, glistening with lotion. With a skillful motion, they caressed his glans. He moaned with pleasure, and she elicited more sounds from the instrument.

Still, it occurred to Michael with horror that she was not *really* playing a coherent song, because for that he would eventually have to sigh, hum, and moan continuously from sheer… She pushed his cock down with considerable force onto the fairly hard stool and the foil taut across it. He groaned in alarm. She played. She took her foot away, the relief bringing forth deep, grateful sounds, alternating with a staccato of pleasure as she played only his glans with her toes. A mean kick, delivered with well-measured force, made him squeal indignantly, allowing the ascent of a frivolous scale. She stroked, kicked, and squeezed his rock-hard cock. By her hands, his whimpering became a hymn. The ladies of the house, struck with utter silence, gazed at the golden slave and Lady Selina. Her bare foot moved in his crotch, kicking and pulling, tickling and twisting. Like a pianist working the pedals of her instrument, Selina manipulated the painful, lustful, fearful sounds Michael emitted. Her fingers stroked and plucked the harp, giving melody to the guttural sounds.

From the sound, the strain in his arms and jaw grew an agony descending into an ecstatic trance. Selina's fingers made the strings vibrate in his teeth, and her foot in his crotch brought him closer to a woeful climax fraught with fear of failure. Her gaze bound his. She did not speak, but threatened, enticed, and rewarded him with the eagerness in her shining eyes. She ungently played with his testicles; soft needle pricks drove through his abdomen, followed by a tender touch that released and, at the same time, tortured him with the torment of an orgasm drawing nearer and nearer. Selina smiled sweetly. Michael, meanwhile, was breathing heavily. Sweat ran from his forehead, chest, and thighs. The gold flowed from his body in glistening trails. Selina's toe tapped cheekily against his reddened glans, rotating it like a joystick. His left arm began to tremble. She noticed it and shook her head slowly, smiling wickedly. A drop of sweat ran down the corner of Michael's eye, and he had to close it. She laughed softly, which only he could hear, and let the song of his pain rise to a triumphant pitch, growing faster and faster until the notes chased and tumbled over one another in the style of Grieg's ever accelerating "Bergkönig." A staccato of fear, excitement, bliss, and pain ended on a high note, at the conclusion of which Lady Selina rose to her feet.

Michael was in a state better described as delirium than trance, his cock screaming for orgasm, his voice hoarse and his entire body trembling. His sweat had trailed the gold off his body in streaks. His jaw was quivering. Only his fear of punishment, his desire not to spoil Lady Selina's masterpiece, kept his body from screaming for release in so many different ways. He took a deep breath. Applause erupted, along with wild cheers and clinking champagne glasses. For one last moment, Selina's face returned, looked him in the eye with a smile, and winked. A hand rose, and the applause ended abruptly. Her finger touched the outermost string on the left and slowly traversed over to the last string on the right. An agonizingly slow, intense, and loud scale sounded.

The last vibration was enough to send a welcome tremor through his body. He gave a muffled cry with the piece of wood in his mouth, tightened the strings once more with a final effort, and surrendered to the humiliating climax witnessed by numerous eyes. The gold- and sweat-smeared instrument poured its seed onto the plastic and the floor in front of the stool. Lady Selina turned around, smiling broadly, and received overwhelming applause for this finale.

"Quite a virtuoso," Janice judged.

Michael stared at the floor, mouth open and eyes widened. Semen dripped from his cock, staining the foil on the stool and the parquet between Selina's feet. Her left foot was smeared with the golden ointment, lovely little footprints showing where she had trudged along awkwardly with only one shoe since his release to accept praise for the performance. He looked up, his strained neck protesting the movement, and an exhausted sigh crept from his lips. Selina accepted more congratulations, shook hands and gave hugs, tipping and tapping only a few inches from him. A hand from the crowd handed her a slender glass. As she reached for it, an endearing "Whoops!" escaped her as she nearly slipped on the lotion on her foot.

A disgrace.

Michael groaned softly. His arms burned with exertion; his knees trembled. With his chest quivering, he straightened up. His seed had flowed out of him, but his energy, his will, and – by Nemesis! – his pride and concern had not.

Only one person in the bulging, chatter-filled salon noticed the gold-smeared slave crawl off the no less smeared stool and approach Lady Selina on all fours. Her otherworldly hair rippled with the unconscious, affirmative nod this sight elicited from her. Michael's hands pulled him forward, his gaze glued to Selina's legs. *Good boy.* The remnants of the lotion made crawling a slippery balancing act, his knees, elbows, and palms unable to find footing. With muscle power alone, he fought back against the danger of slipping. In vain.

Michael had almost reached Selina when his left leg lost grip. He must have put his knee on a spot already wet with lotion or semen, because he slipped, and the incipient plopping sound and his strained whimper made Selina and a handful of ladies take notice.

"Oh, sweetheart," Selina hummed, bending down to him, her foot, stained with golden ointment, placed quite haphazardly next to his head. "Be a good boy and stay on your stool. You were great," she serenaded, stroking his hair. "We don't need you anymore today, but you may stay there and be ogled by all the lovely ladies. Huh? Sounds good?"

Michael gasped, braced his palms on the parquet and heaved his upper body in Selina's direction. She watched him, fascinated. He put his lips on her bare foot and kissed it, sighing, relieved and grateful. She put her head back with an endearing smile, and the ladies all around gushed in a touched "Aww, cute!" Michael's tongue slipped out of its socket and licked Selina's pretty, dainty toes, covered in dirty gold. It was as much an act of worship as it was a cleansing. The remnants of the lotion tasted bland and empty on his tongue, the faint scent lost in the taste of Selina's skin and the hint of salt on it. Selina caressed his back, allowing his unrestrained kissing and licking. "You are a wonderful slave, Michael," she sighed.

The better life. Peter sighed, closed the door behind him, and put his messenger bag on the sideboard. He hung his jacket on the fancy coat rack, Luisa's choice, and caught it as it fell from the nearly unusable – but beautifully curved

– hooks. He hung it up again, more carefully this time. He repeated his sigh and went to the kitchen. He was drained and tired from the afternoon he had stolen to help Ms. Jana and the ladies of the house.

His smartphone vibrated. Peter hadn't paid attention to it all afternoon and raised it in front of his face, chewing on a sandwich with lots of mayonnaise, ham, and cheese melted in the microwave. He swiped aside six push notifications from his soccer app, the news, and his pedometer ("Keep it up, your step count has been going up for nine days!") and read his text messages. Lo and behold, Luisa had texted him.

"The fact that you don't reach out speaks of volumes," she had stated.

Peter snorted, answering succinctly, "Right. It's just volumes, btw."

The next message was from Maurice, a coworker in IT, asking for the name of a series Peter had mentioned a few weeks ago. He answered and moved on to the last message.

"How much do you make?" Ms. Jana had asked fifteen minutes ago.

"Are you trying to headhunt me?" he replied.

Ms. Jana promptly replied, "Come to the house on Saturday. Not a business meeting. 7 p.m. Suit and tie." This announcement was followed by two winking emojis.

Peter sighed a third time.

As you wish, Ms. Jana.

Peter drove through the archway and stepped on the brakes without hesitation. The gravel-strewn driveway was lined with dozens of torches flickering in the balmy breeze of the summer evening. A young security guard in a tuxedo stepped out from behind the open gate and held up a clipboard. Peter lowered the window.

"Good evening, are you lost?" the young man asked, looking skeptically at Peter's station wagon.

Peter shook his head and gave his name. "I was invited by Ms. Jana at 7 p.m."

His interlocutor crossed out a name far up on the clipboard. "Ah, Mr. Wartmann. Please forgive me. We're expecting mostly female visitors, and you wouldn't be the first to arrive here hoping for a U-turn."

Peter nodded. "Do… I have to park somewhere separately?"

The guard shook his head. "There's a valet waiting for you upstairs."

Peter snorted. "Wow, like at the Casino Royale. But what's going on tonight? A party?"

The security guard cleared his throat in irritation at this apparently very silly question and looked up at the brightly lit house. "An auction."

A parking attendant accepted Peter's car keys and drove away in routine fashion. Peter uneasily smoothed out his suit. The thumping of two high heels sounded behind him as he gazed after his station wagon, which absolutely did not match the atmosphere. A mysterious black sedan would have looked good now.

Assuming the heels thumping behind him on the stairs belonged to Ms. Jana, he picked up on one of their little inside jokes before turning around. "You know, the supervillain always gets rid of James Bond's car just as elegantly before he invites him into his casino or grand hotel built for money laundering."

An unfamiliar voice chuckled. "Whoa, right, so cliché

with the parking attendants you casually toss the car keys to n' stuff! You should have told him 'Don't scratch the paintjob, laddie!'"

Peter spun around. A petite blonde woman in a black formal dress waved at him from the landing of the stairs. He had seen her before. But where? "Excuse me," he asked, "I assumed you were Ms. Jana."

The pretty blonde shook her head, introduced herself as "Carlotta," and curtsied politely, lifting the flowing skirt of her dress with pointed fingers.

Peter gave a bow with a grin. "Peter Wartmann. I've been invited."

She smiled broadly. "I know. I get to entertain you until the big show starts. Please follow me."

He huffed and climbed the steps. Carlotta was petite and looked up at him from ice blue eyes. "Entertain me?" he asked with raised eyebrows.

She mimicked his facial expression cheekily and purred with emphasis, "Entertain you, Mr. Wartmann. Scrabble, UNO, Battleship, and Jenga. I got all the good stuff." He snorted, and she grabbed his wrist. "Come on, Mr. Wartmann! I'm sooo happy we're finally getting to hang out."

Maybe it was her perfume or her swaying movement as she turned and pulled him through the familiar entrance hall, but Peter suddenly remembered where he had seen Carlotta before. "You brought us coffee, during our first meeting," he said.

Her blonde bob bounced eagerly. "Ah, you remember. I must have made an impression," she teased. She still held him by the wrist, and Peter felt silly being escorted like this. She dragged him through the first floor, past the white staircase that led down to the swimming pool before branching off into a carpeted hallway. Was Carlotta also a mistress in this house?

He cleared his throat. "So… there's one of the famed auctions tonight?"

Carlotta nodded and opened one of the magnificent, whitewashed doors. "That's right" – she pointed into the room – "Please do enter, Mr. Wartmann. You are an honorary guest." He took a deep breath, braced himself for whatever sight might await him in this room, and stepped inside.

It was a chicly furnished salon full of armchairs, couches, and sofas. The furniture was all oriented toward a huge flat-screen TV on the wall, and small side tables provided space for snacks and drinks. Peter had seen playrooms and bedrooms and bathrooms and offices in this house before. This room, he thought, seemed downright civil.

"This is where we watch series together," Carlotta said with a smirk.

He turned to the young woman. "Very glamorous."

She opened her hands with a grin. "Choose a seat, Mr. Wartmann. We will be joined by other viewers. The auction will be shown on the screen via livestream. I hope you understand that you cannot be present in the actual auction room. It is an intimate act."

Peter obeyed and sat down on one of the sofas, far in front, close to the television. "Understandable. Who is being auctioned off, then? I've already had a very enlightening conversation with the gentleman called Fourteen. Tobias Roudette."

Carlotta winked. "That's him. He's the most important exhibit in today's auction. Before him, Seventeen, the next in line, will be advertised as a future available product. However, he' s not ready yet." She stepped up to the large screen and awkwardly pressed a button far overhead that activated it. A remote control found its way into her hand, and after two channel changes and a few seconds of blackness, a theater stage appeared on the screen. Silhouettes of elaborate hairdos floated across the bottom of the screen. Every now and then, a slender female hand waved at someone outside the visible area. Peter's eyes snapped open. A round red mattress lay in the middle of the stage, and a couple was having reckless sex on it.

"Is…" he stammered, "Is this live?" The woman wrapped her legs around the man's butt.

Carlotta nodded casually. "Yes, it's the opening act. The male slave's name is Smoothie, and this pretty one here is Apple. I like Smoothie, even though in the heat of the moment he sometimes forgets that breasts still exist after foreplay. I've never had Apple yet, but Selina says she's totally sweet. I would have rather let Kiwi do Apple. He's a bit wilder, but not in a self-absorbed way. Anyway, Derya got to decide. Won at rock, paper, scissors." She wrinkled her pretty nose. "Who the hell takes paper three times in a row and wins with it, for crying out loud?"

Peter sat with his jaw hanging open. "They… have sex in front of an audience there," he stated dryly, unable to take his eyes off the frantically fucking couple on the red mattress.

Carlotta smiled. "Sure! We can hardly show the guests porn on a screen, Mr. Wartmann." She snorted. "They're accustomed to better."

The door to the media room opened, and another lady entered. She was considerably older than Carlotta and wore a formal suit in charcoal gray. Compared to Carlotta's evening gown, it could easily have looked dull, but an opulent, glittering brooch on her lapel and an outrageously large pearl necklace elevated the suit into the realm of skillfully applied splendor. The woman had tied her hair into a severe bun, which bestowed her with something of a governess. Long pearl earrings, falling almost to her shoulders, complemented the jewelry on her neck. In Peter, the sight of her abruptly triggered the bewildered humility of someone clueless at a fashion show, someone who could make sense of the designer's name but clammily wondered how an ordinary person would ever wear such a thing.

"Lady Janice," she introduced herself and extended her

hand to Peter, who had politely stood up.

He abruptly felt he had to bow. "Peter Wartmann, delighted to meet you."

Janice pulled up one side of her mouth and glanced briefly in Carlotta's direction. "'Delighted.' How sweetly put. The pleasure is all mine," she said.

Peter didn't know what had prompted him to use the old-fashioned greeting, but he returned her smile. "'Delighted' absolutely sums it up. This is the first time I've met any ladies of the house other than Ms. Jana."

Janice nodded emphatically. "No reason to be shy about the cats here," she recommended with a wink, wiping a piece of lint from Peter's shoulder. "They'll bite either way." She sat down in a white armchair the shape of a seashell, positioned behind Peter, and examined her face in a small makeup mirror.

Carlotta settled next to Peter, awkwardly gathering the hem of her dress. "Whew, so," she squeaked, sinking into the cushions, "I totally loved your design for the website."

Peter smiled. "Thank you. It is – if I may say so – forcedly simple."

Janice snorted behind them, "I know a few people you could say the same about." The three laughed cheerfully, as if there wasn't the wildest sex taking place on the screen, sex that Peter could only dream of actually physically performing.

He cleared his throat and felt a blush creep into his cheeks. "Well, what I mean by that is, Ms. Jana has the ambition to address exactly the right target audience with a single page. No pillar pages, and little text in which I can place important keywords. The site is challenging in a great way."

Carlotta nodded understandingly. "That's exactly what I thought. Usually there's a lot more text on a home page like this, and at the top, there's some kind of navigation with things like 'About us' and 'Our product' and 'The team,' and so on."

Peter was genuinely delighted at her prescience. "Exactly! The page for the house, on the other hand, will just be a header, some text, and a—"

Again the door opened. A beautiful middle eastern woman in a flowing dress entered, smiling. Peter rose again. The lady caught sight of him, and her smile widened. "The web specialist?"

He nodded. "Peter Wartmann. Good evening."

She introduced herself as Lady Derya, and her lovely, round face beamed. She was, unlike petite Carlotta and tall Janice, of medium height and possessed quite extraordinary curves that accentuated her flowing dress. "I'm in charge of the kitchen here," she explained tersely. "I teach the servants how to cook and make sure they know a Riesling from a Bordeaux."

Peter marveled, "This house thinks of everything. Impressive."

Derya tilted her head conspiratorially. "My exhaustion of cooking spoons is, as Ms. Jana likes to put it, the main reason for the high prices of our products."

Peter bristled. "Do the gentlemen treat the kitchen utensils so badly?" The three ladies unexpectedly laughed.

"Misappropriation, Mr. Wartmann," Janice explained, tracing her lipstick. "An awful lot in this house is based on deliberate misappropriation."

Into the resounding laughter of the good-humored women, the door opened again. Peter met a lady named Tatjana, who wore a pantsuit embroidered with subtle brilliants. Her slender, sinewy feet stood in elegant high heels, her nails painted white. She sat down next to Derya, likewise behind the couch that Peter and the pretty Carlotta had claimed for themselves.

A guttural scream of pleasure from the slave Apple on the screen, coming from the depths of her body, marked the beginning of the end in the pre-auction program. She basked in the warm showers of an intense orgasm while the slave named Smoothie pulled his cock out of her and began rubbing it. Apple sighed deeply and straightened her upper body, mouth open wide and lascivious, eyes rolling ecstatically upward in their sockets. Smoothie – what an obscene name in this particular context – brought himself to climax, spurting his cum into the open mouth of his playmate. She drank uninhibitedly and gratefully. White splotches landed on her chin, neck, and chest. The silhouettes of several hands rose at the bottom of the screen, offering polite applause. Smoothie lay down next to Apple, and three stark naked men appeared from backstage and pushed the bed, along with the red mattress and the two people on it, out of the picture.

Peter shook his head in bewilderment. To see the absolutely obscure sexual implicitness in this house with his own eyes was something completely different than to hear stories from the cultivated lips of Ms. Jana.

The dry click of high heels on hard parquet sounded. The lights went out except for a single cone of light in the center of the stage. The hands silenced their applause, and the impressive updos stopped moving as a tense silence settled over the auditorium. Only the sound of approaching heels resounded in the darkness. Then such a sublime, unnaturally beautiful figure stepped into the beams of the last spotlight that Peter abruptly took a deep breath. Ms. Jana had entered the stage.

Her vivid-looking hair fell over her shoulders. Her eyes shone down on the audience in an almost surreal tone of amber. She wore a dark blue dress with slim sleeves reaching her wrists. An elegant slit showed enough of her legs to impress with physical beauty, yet not to overwhelm. It was followed by a short train that cascaded in waves, quite intentionally breaking with the ceremonial seriousness of the dress. Ms. Jana wore – the slit allowed a hint of a glimpse – open-toed high heels that cast themselves into elaborate leather ornaments graced with small, glittering stones on the tops of her feet.

She opened her hands, and a soft, knowing smile slid

onto her face. "Good evening, ladies."

Peter wished he could have turned to Lady Carlotta and asked where all the bidders had come from, but Jana kept talking, and he didn't want to miss any of her words.

"We are happy to have you all gathered here. We are proud to *be able to* gather you all here. The last event of this kind took place two years ago, as some of you remember. It fills my staff and me with great pleasure to see this hall full of tense anticipation once again, to bask in the opportunity to welcome you as guests in my house and to present you the fruits of our labor. Our house lives on you, ladies. Therefore, allow us to show you not only the ripe, but also the *still growing* fruits. You are bidding on the wonderful Fourteen today. He is a masterpiece, I assure you. The path into the lap of a good owner has been long and hard for him, and yes, we have turned down many an offer, many a request to come here and bid on him. You are all here because you are worthy of Fourteen, because you may own Fourteen, ladies.

"Before our most important exhibit enters the stage, we would like to prove to you that the training in our company is still incomparable to anything else in the world. To quote none less than Aristotle, 'Learning never exhausts the mind.' An apprenticeship with us" – something eerie crept into her gaze, and for a moment, she fixed the camera above the audience and looked Peter directly in the eye – "surely exhausts the body."

The audience laughed wisely. Lady Carlotta's hand grasped Peter's, and he turned his head in surprise. "Hey, face forward," she purred, and he obeyed.

Lady Jana bowed. "Please enjoy the demonstration featuring my dear colleague Lady Selina and Seventeen, our next product, which will be ready in a few years."

Two naked slave girls brought something onto the stage which, at first, reminded Peter of a shiny chrome pole in a strip club and inserted it into a specially made contraption in the floor. A soft click sounded, and the slave girls took several steps back and knelt on the parquet with their heads down. Peter swallowed and felt blood rush to his loins at the sight of the naked women. High heels sounded again, and another woman, a mane of raven black hair on her head, led a muscular young man on a dog leash into the spotlights. *Lady Selina*, Peter concluded. She lacked Ms. Jana's elegance, but where her superior shone sublimely, Selina burned searingly hot. She wore a snow-white blouse with pale gold frills at the shoulders and sleeves. Her legs stuck in black leather pants, the hem disappeared into boots that left both her toes and heel uncovered. Seventeen, the product-to-be, wore nothing at all except the collar to which the leash he was wearing was attached. Selina slowly led him across the stage. How frightened and excited he had to be!

When Selina reached the silver bar with her tantalizingly slow gait, she tied Seventeen's leash to it and positioned the slave with his back to the audience. "On your knees, head down," she said loudly. He obeyed, and Peter found that his own knees were shaking as much as those of the young man. Selina turned to the audience. She raised an arm, and one of the slave girls jumped up. "A number between 1 and 10," Selina asked the audience. *No answer.* She grinned as the slave returned with a long black whip and placed it in Selina's outstretched hand.

"Eight," a voice with an indefinable accent eventually said.

Selina smiled. "Thank you, my lady. Eight it is."

The audience, including Peter, assumed this was about calling a number of lashes to be administered and was surprised at the low figure. Selina let the whip snap across the floor in a menacing, snake-like manner. "Eight, as you wish," she purred, and the whip sprang forth without warning, snapping at the slave's hunched back and describing a ghastly arc between the shoulder blades. Seventeen flinched but suppressed any cry with bewildering routine. Selina corrected her position by half a step, cracked the whip in the air once, and then brought it down from a different angle with a twist of her wrist. Another vicious blow struck him just above the buttocks. A sharp intake of breath sounded.

Peter flinched noticeably. Carlotta giggled beside him.

Only the whip could be heard in the absolute silence of the hall as it came down a third time on Seventeen, drawing an almost straight line from upper left to lower right. An identical stroke from the opposite direction completed an imaginary X on his back. Selina turned and smiled at the audience. At first, a few heads turned back and forth in confusion at this expertly executed, yet – for *the house* – very ordinary performance. Besides, wasn't it supposed to be eight strokes? It took a moment for the puzzled glances to make an astonishing discovery on the slave's martyred back.

Peter groaned audibly, "That…"

The skin reddened. Within a minute, a large, sinister figure eight appeared on Seventeen's back. The X formed the spot where the lines crossed. The blow between the shoulders and just above the buttocks had created two perfect semicircles that closed it.

Astonished murmurs rose. Selina tilted her head with a grin and flicked her finger. The second slave rose and hurried off the stage. Selina approached Seventeen and grasped his head. She whispered something to him. He nodded, trembling. The slave returned with a glass of clear liquid. Selina accepted it and dumped it out over Seventeen's back. A shrill scream rippled through the hall, and Peter flinched instinctively. The audience applauded.

"Alcohol," Carlotta whispered, resting her head against Peter's shoulder. "Vodka, I think."

Selina tapped against Seventeen's shaking shoulders. He rose to his feet. She turned him around with a grip on his hip. The ladies laughed and applauded enthusiastically; he had an erection. Selina downed the rest of the vodka and stuck the glass on Seventeen's cock as if on a holder.

"Thank you!" she announced in several languages. "Merci! Danke! Grazie!"

"Well, was that good or was that good?" Lady Selina asked.

Michael nodded eagerly. "You were great, Lady Selina. I even twitched back here when you cracked the whip!"

She laughed and caressed the slender slave's cheek. "Help me into something more festive," she purred, undoing the top button of her blouse herself. They were backstage in a dressing room, where Michael waited obediently for Selina. He had been smitten with her ever since she had played the harp and sighed sweetly at her touch.

The terrible word "broken" had imposed itself, but the ladies of the house did not think so. Michael followed Selina wherever she wanted, and the beautiful mistress enjoyed her little slave. He raised his hands and touched the zipper of her boot but hesitated for a moment. His gaze was glued to the three cute toes that cheekily peeked out of the opening below.

Selina giggled and ruffled his hair. "All right, but only because it's you, my wabbit."

Michael gave her a grateful canine look before his head sank to the floor. He closed his lips around the toe opening of her boots and his tongue slid over her toes. He sighed happily. She opened her blouse herself. He inhaled deeply through his mouth, soaked up her scent, and began licking her toes in a disinhibited, dog-like manner. She let it happen, stripped off her blouse, and folded it conscientiously. "The other one," she murmured, switching her foot under Michael's mouth. He whimpered gratefully, and his lips gave her boot and feet small, lovely kisses.

Selina's burgundy evening gown hung on the coat rack, and she eyed it impatiently. She finally withdrew her second foot from him as well and hastily tapped against her thigh. "Enough, slave. Help me out of my clothes now."

He raised his torso and prepared to remove her boots. This was done with ritual seriousness, and Michael placed them both neatly side by side, running longing glances over the high shaft. Selina now stood before him in stunning lingerie. Michael's penis ached in its pink plastic cage. "My dress."

He looked over to the dresser and she nodded, giving permission to stand.

The two naked slave girls had wiped the vodka stains from the stage and retreated. The lights died again. The almost ethereal figure of Ms. Jana returned. She was followed by a handsome, strong, yet not too accentuated, muscular man who walked upright. His cheeky curls shimmered in the dim light, and a mischievous smile did indeed cross his face. Heads turned back and forth. Fourteen looked great. Ms. Jana brushed over his shoulder.

"Ladies: Tobias Roudette. Fourteen."

Peter gulped. He liked the man, and he hoped a gorgeous lady would bid for him. "And if his buyer," he whispered to Carlotta, who was leaning against his shoulder with youthful insolence and just as much self-evidence, "is not to his liking?"

The young mistress giggled and pinched his chest. "Silly! He helped select the attendees. Only ladies he can absolutely picture himself being with are sitting here."

Fourteen bowed and got down on one knee before Ms. Jana put a blindfold on him and inserted two discreet earplugs. Peter furrowed his brow.

Carlotta patted his thigh and replied before he could ask, "It's an empirical thing. The ladies don't want him to witness the battle of the bidders around him. It wouldn't be beneficial to the new mistress' dominance if her slave saw her flailing her arms frantically in greed. And the slave shouldn't know his own price. It's not good for a young relationship to know how much the mistress has paid for the slave. Afterwards, of course, she can tell him. We can't prevent that, but we don't recommend it."

Jana's heart pounded violently. She would gladly have whispered to Fourteen how much she wished a wonderful lady for him, how much she wished him happiness, how much she would miss his clever mind in her house. He nodded imperceptibly, as if sensing the words not said.

The single spotlight dimmed, and the others began to shine again. She could see the ladies present for the first time. There were six good-looking women dressed as if for an aristocratic wedding present in the great hall. Two had been to previous auctions and knew Jana. Good women, but they had ultimately decided against bidding for the slave of that time or were no longer able to bid. Fourteen had chosen the women well. She would gladly let any one of them have her living masterpiece, as different as their tempers present were. Each of them corresponded with a part of Tobias Roudette's character. Each of them needed him. Each could offer him something he lacked.

"Fourteen," she piped up. "Tobias Roudette. In the house for six years. Finished his education two years ago. Speaks five languages, the native languages of those present included. Classical vocal training. Plays violin, piano, and four woodwind instruments with virtuosity. Physical endurance sufficient for a marathon with excellent times for a non-professional athlete. No health problems, no injuries in the past, a negligible allergy to a single spring flower excluded. Penis length of 18.2 centimeters. Writes poems and goes by the pseudonym Lars Skolhart, who wrote the thriller *Clear Cut*, a bestseller in nine countries, published in 2021. Master of Science in economics. Expertise in sales controlling and marketing." She stood in front of her product and looked at each of the captivated women. "Ladies, in Fourteen, you'll find the best product since the slave named Zero, our most gifted outlier from two years ago."

A murmur went through the audience, both in the auction room and in the media salon. Janice whistled appreciatively. "She's gambling high."

Carlotta had lifted her head from Peter's shoulder and unconsciously squeezed his hand. He looked at the petite blonde. "Zero?"

She stared at the screen, smiling. "Was before my time, I'm afraid. A man like a myth. The perfect slave. He was brought here by a world-famous lady who no longer works in the business. Not trained here, but using our methods. He arrived, his owner said goodbye, and the same evening the auction took place. Jana and Selina know the sum he yielded but never mention it."

"The lowest bid is," Jana said, trying hard not to stutter or hesitate. "One million."

Gasps and sharp intakes of breath all around. Peter straightened up on the sofa. Heels clicked behind him as many a relaxingly crossed leg found its way back to the floor.

Carlotta shook her head in fascination. "She is going all in."

One of the updos rose silently and left the auction room. Two other women were visibly toying with the idea of doing the same. "Signora Jana" – one voice raised and switched to English, while five pointed fingers slid into view in the typical Italian gesture of outrage, wagging threateningly – "Are you outta your mind?"

"La mia testa sta bene, Padrona," Jana replied politely, folding her arms behind her back. "He's worth it."

A hand rose in the darkness. "A million and ten thousand," announced a high, endearing voice.

An unfathomable clamor broke out in the media salon. Peter jumped in fright as Carlotta shrieked in unbridled delight, wrenching her arms, and his hand right along with them, into the air. "They're bidding, Nemesis! They're bidding!"

Lady Derya literally tumbled over the back of Peter's sofa and hugged Carlotta from behind. The blonde bounced up and down, dragging Peter's arm with her. Tatjana joined them in a roar, and they formed a tangle of jubilant women in formal dress and an overwhelmed SEO specialist, elbows, knees and hips smacking his face.

Lady Janice, shaking her head but grinning broadly at the same time, looked over at the younger ladies who had buried Peter beneath them.

Jana nodded with a smile and repeated, "A million and ten thousand."

The Italian lady cursed profusely, "Twenty thousand! But I'll bring him back if he can't fuck three nights straight without a break. Nemesis, I swear, these monopolists around here…"

Jana repeated this sum as well. Another lady rose and took her leave with a courtly curtsy. Jana acknowledged this with a silent nod of her head. The ladies had bid; Fourteen would be sold.

"Thirty thousand," said a third voice.

"Forty," replied the first.

"One million and one hundred thousand! Suck it up, bitches!" the Italian woman sneered, making the media salon on the other side of the building laugh frenetically. Jana visibly struggled to contain her amusement.

Silence ensued. Jana looked at each of the ladies.

"You better not open your mouths!" the Italian woman's voice ruled.

Ms. Jana laughed softly.

"One hundred and ten thousand," whispered the first bidder defiantly. Peter thought he could literally see the Padrona's eye roll.

"Fifteen," she barked back.

"Twenty," came the reply.

"Do you wanna mess with me, sweetie?" the padrona

asked with a loud sigh, rising to her feet. For the first time, Peter actually saw her face instead of a fancy high hairdo and was startled to recognize the Oscar-winning actress Gianna diMesa, whom he had marveled at just last month in her role as Dolores Camezzini in *Burning Skies*. "I've got stamina and a bank account fatter than the husband you had to kill for your auction budget."

"You understand why the slave shouldn't necessarily listen in on the auction?" Carlotta brushed Peter's lapel with a lovely twinkle in her eye.

He nodded with a snort. "Perfectly."

"Do you speak from experience, dear?" the first lady asked, rising as well. While her lovely face told Peter nothing, he could tell from the reaction of Lady Derya, who was still standing next to him, that she was well known among the ladies.

"Elizabeth Cartwright," she whispered. Peter looked up at the beautiful mistress.

"Cartwright? As in Cartwright Airlines 'Fly anywhere, but in style'?"

Derya nodded. Peter sighed hard.

Into the aggressive silence, Ms. Jana's voice announced, "One million and one hundred twenty thousand. To the first."

The audience in the media salon held its breath. "To the second."

"Thirty," said the Italian woman.

All heads turned to the airline owner. She sighed.

Carlotta grabbed Peter's arm. " Almost…"

"Let's wrap this up," Elizabeth Cartwright sighed, locking eyes with her adversary. "One million and two hundred thousand."

"To the first," Jana announced.

Gianna diMesa puffed her cheeks in frustration and

waved it off. "Let her have him. Congratulations."

Jana nodded. "To the second."

No one raised their voices.

"To the third." She yanked the blindfold from Fourteen's head. "Sold to Lady Elizabeth!"

The ladies broke into renewed cheers. Carlotta hugged the surprised Peter as if they had known each other for years. Derya bent down to give Carlotta a hug, at which point Tatjana, crashing over all three of them, knocked them over and again they became a jubilant whirl of dresses, arms, and legs that rolled on the sofa.

Janice rose silently, lit a cigarette, and watched the screen where Jana was politely applauding the lucky winner. As if sensing the gaze of her oldest companion, the mistress of the house raised her head and looked into the small camera above the last row.

Janice nodded.

Jana smiled subtly.

CHAPTER 7: ACCEPTING COOKIES

"Let go of the poor man," Janice said, tenderly caressing Derya's shoulder. The three younger women, faces flushed, obeyed the domina and rose from the sofa, smoothing their clothes. Still, each had a wild grin on her face.

Tatjana cleared her throat in embarrassment. "That's… an incredible price."

Carlotta nodded. "Fourteen just gave us years of financial stability."

Derya excitedly snapped her finger and pointed at Tatjana. "We can modernize the spa!"

Before the three ladies began to entertain ideas, Janice grabbed the shoulders of Peter Wartmann, who was sitting between them, looking uneasy. "These proceeds provide financial backing," she explained, kneading his shoulders determinedly, "until the site is up and running. The money allows us to invest."

Peter raised his head uncertainly and tried to look Janice, who was standing behind him, "I pledged my help to Ms. Jana, Lady Janice. Even if I were here with the agency, such an astronomical price would never be charged for a single website of this category. I…" – he attempted a confident smile – "am helping because I want to help."

"Wanting to help is great," said a friendly voice behind them. Five heads whirled round and caught sight of Lady Selina in the doorway. She had swapped her blouse and leather pants for a flaming red evening gown. "But after all, you must eat," she said, coming closer, "Drink, bathe, and shop. Besides, you should set aside a tiny bit for... retirement, don't you think?" She sat down next to Peter and ran her hand over his back. Peter remained silent, perplexed.

Selina smiled sweetly. "Ms. Jana would like to talk to you, Mr. Wartmann."

Peter merely nodded.

Lady Janice stroked his shoulder. "So eager to help, *Mister Search Engine...*"

"Whoa, are you naming a robot or what? That's way too lengthy!" complained Carlotta.

Peter, understanding less and less, turned to her. "Excuse me?"

The blonde put a finger to his lips and just shook her head, winking. "Imagine him standing right in line with the others and then we've got Cheeky, Smoothie, Crumble, Muffin, Footsy, T-Bone, Dip, and *Mister Search Engine.*"

Derya snorted. "Correct."

Janice opened her hands in an irritated gesture. "Go ahead, I'm open to ideas."

Peter frowned. *What the...?*

Selina tidied the collar of his shirt, which had suffered from the ladies' joyous attacks. "*Suit,*" she purred as she did so. "Because he fits."

Tatjana stroked his head. "He doesn't always wear one, though. I'm all for *Crunchy*. Number-crunching while analyzing and calculating, you know? Or *Numbers*, for that matter!"

Peter let the naughty touches wash over him. "*Keyword,*" Derya interjected, to which Janice retorted, "*Techno.*" The irritated looks from the others that followed this straight-out-of-the-90s suggestion made the oldest of the ladies throw her arms up in the air in frustration. "All right, kiddos, I'll shut up already. Take what you want."

Lady Elizabeth had brought a wonderful tuxedo for her purchase, which Fourteen donned in the middle of the stage of the theater hall. The other bidders had retired to one of the festively prepared salons, where comforting champagne, a delicate buffet, and numerous willing servants of the house awaited them. The ladies of Jana's inner circle would soon join them for expert talks on the proper upbringing of servants and perhaps a demonstration or two on the live object. Fourteen tied the bow tie expertly and looked up into Elizabeth's face with a smile. His new owner beamed. "You look wonderful, handsome."

Jana nodded. "Quite excellent."

Fourteen turned to face her. There was a faint sadness in his gaze. She gently stroked his cheek. "We'll miss you, Fourteen. But we take comfort in knowing that in Lady Elizabeth you have found the best owner imaginable."

The pretty American sighed. "I am overjoyed to have bought him."

Michael was shaking all over. A stunningly beautiful woman with dark brown hair had barged into the salon, slapped him at random, and toppled two glasses of champagne. Four other ladies were already seated at the many tables, two chatting with each other, the other two enjoying a foot massage from the slaves present. One of them settled down for this same treatment on one of the large, decadent couches. A slave fed her grapes, completing the image of the ancient Caesaress. Michael had the pleasure of serving the dark-haired fury, who had given him the aforementioned slap and ignored him ever since. He was a good slave. He was brave.

"M-more champagne, Mistress?" he asked in a trembling voice. The woman turned and focused on him with a look he wished could kill, for the threats therein were worse than dropping dead on the spot. She stared at him like a lioness about to pounce. Michael stared back, dazed and afraid.

As if struck with a sledgehammer, a realization hit him. "Mistress, you," he stammered, "are Gianna diMesa. I saw you at the Academy Awards." *And masturbated to photos of your feet I found on Instagram*, he added in thought. She tilted her head gradually, in slow motion, and Michael corrected the image in his mind's eye from a cat to a snake, approaching its prey with writhing, soundless movements until it could squirt its venom.

"Sí," she finally hissed. "I'm Gianna diMesa."

He raised the champagne bottle in a very hopeful gesture. "More champagne, Mistress Gianna?"

Her fearsome silence returned. She regarded him quietly.

He lowered the bottle and his head in a moment. "Forgive me, Mistress Gianna."

Her finger slid slowly to his chin and lifted his head again. "Yes," she purred, "More champagne is a great idea."

Peter had already registered that the lady named Janice exercised some authority over the other four. She had, when the odd discussion about a suitable nickname for him threatened to fizzle out, clapped her hands resolutely. "Up, my dears. I'm sure Ms. Jana would appreciate our presence in the dining room. We have international guests to entertain."

They all rose. Only petite Carlotta paused and took Peter's hand. "I'll take you to Jana's office, Mr. SEO Guy," she said in an endearingly awkward way, offset by a broad smile. "I'm the one responsible for you, after all."

Peter returned her smile. "Thank you very much.

However, I can find my own way there. This is not my first time here, Ms. Carlotta."

She grinned. "I know. But today is special," she decided.

Gianna snatched the bottle from Michael, took a long swig, and then shoved the neck of the bottle down his throat. "Bevi, mio schiavo," she hissed. *Drink, my slave.* And Michael drank.

Gianna laughed throatily, her hair bobbing in confirmation. "Very good."

When he threatened to choke on the fine champagne, she pulled the bottle from his mouth and flicked unpleasantly against his bare belly. "On your knees," she commanded.

As soon as he knelt, she leaped onto the nearest seat and flung her brilliantly studded stilettos off her feet by two careless motions. "Over here. You're very thirsty, slave."

Michael crawled in front of her chair, and she lifted a foot. "Open your mouth. There's drinking to be had, footboy."

He opened his mouth to receive her fragrant toes, sweaty with anger, excitement, and uncomfortable footwear. She held up the champagne bottle, and the other guests laughed and applauded. Michael knew what was about to happen and sighed happily. How many men had gushed about Gianna diMesa's beautiful feet, how many celebrity foot forums were brimming with praise for the superstar who was such a big hit with fetish fans? How many guys took screenshots of her social media posts when even the tip of a high heel peeked out from under her skirt? In a moment, he'd be drinking champagne from the world's most coveted toes.

Hand in hand with Carlotta, Peter strode down the jade green carpeted hallway that led toward Ms. Jana's office.

The bubbly blonde snuggled up to him as they walked.

"This is so cool," she hummed. "A really awesome auction, a nice evening with exciting guests, our internet guy finally shows his cute lil' face." She winked.

Peter smiled wanly and self-consciously. "I found the evening very enlightening," he said.

Carlotta laughed brightly. "Now that's a word that can be taken both ways, Peter!"

He shook his head. "I meant it positively. Even if I still hope for your consideration. Seeing it is different than being told about it."

She nodded in understand. "Sure, I totally get it. But then… you *were* one of us before." A question disguised as a cheeky observation.

He cleared his throat. *Yes and no* was the answer. "I, um… I do have a certain, sexual preference…"

She rolled her eyes. "A foot fetish, Peter!"

Well, well, he thought. The ladies knew about it. He could have been angry with Ms. Jana, who had revealed his secret to her coworkers. But he wasn't. It felt good to talk about it with the open minded, fun-loving Carlotta. He felt outed in a good way. The heavy shield in his head, reinforced over many years and supplemented with more hard layers, lowered heavily.

He smiled again. "Yes. I have a foot fetish. I can't deny that I used to consume a lot of foot-related content before I met my ex-girlfriend."

Carlotta laughed out loud and threw her head back. "Consumed foot-related content? Did you eat the videos or something?"

He laughed alongside her. "No, of course not. I used to watch pornography and erotic videos about foot fetish and a bit of female domination. And I did that a lot. Then, as I said, with my relationship with Luisa, that changed. She let me have my" – Carlotta's raised eyebrows made him correct his words – "Luisa *tolerated* my foot fetish."

The blonde snorted. "I can tolerate a neighbor who

gives me a week's notice of a loud house party." Now Peter laughed. Carlotta squeezed his hand tighter. "You're with your own kind now, Peter."

He exhaled softly. He still had full-time employment, an apartment downtown, a toxic ex-girlfriend, a quarter of a crumbling circle of friends, and a bunch of other private business. Carlotta was treating him as if he had decided to work exclusively for the ladies of the house, or even move into the house. "We *accept* you, Peter. Just as you are…" she paused. Her eyes widened, and her lovely mouth opened into an enthusiastic smile. He stared blankly. She seemed to have had a veritable flash of inspiration.

"Is something wrong?"

Carlotta bit her tongue with a grin and stepped closer with a sway of her hips. "We hereby accept this *cookie*," she whispered, kissing him on the mouth without warning. "Don't tell Ms. Jana," she implored him with a raised index finger immediately afterwards.

The cool champagne ran down Michael's face. The liquid splashed left and right from the grinning actress' slender legs, tumbling in lavish torrents into the pits of her tense muscles. Less of the liquid anointed by her fragrant skin than he had hoped landed in his greedily sucking mouth. Gianna laughed at his degrading motions and the pleasure with which he sucked her toes.

"Bravo," she praised, "A good footboy!"

Michael licked the trails of crystalline liquid that threatened to run dry from the top of her foot and sighed gratefully. Gianna finally slumped down in the chair and extended her bare soles, reddened from her high heels, to him. "Relax me, slave. I've had a terrible evening."

Carlotta opened the door to Jana's office. The mistress of the house was not present. "She'll be with you in a moment," the lovely blonde whispered, kissing Peter on the cheek. "She's drawn up a contract, I think."

Peter nodded, nevertheless puzzled. His offer to help the ladies get a fancy website in his spare time had been amicable, not to say *free*, out of sympathy for the absolutely obscure thing that was going here.

"Would," he asked quietly, "Ms. Jana like to entice me away from my employer? She asked me how much I make."

Carlotta looked up at the ceiling, playfully musing, "Hmm. I think she just wants to *tie things up* properly so the work can begin."

Michael's penis struggled against the cage. He licked Gianna diMesa's feet, massaging the soles, pushing her lovely toes apart with discreet force so he could conscientiously lick the spaces between them clean. They smelled of the leather of expensive heeled shoes and remnants of champagne and tasted of a hint of salt. Michael's heart was pounding; his abdomen ached with denied arousal.

The actress had descended upon him. He would have been less baffled if a blue whale had appeared out of nowhere in the house's pond. He licked Gianna's heel, lifting her leg with well-measured force and sliding his tongue along it, making intense, self-forgetting movements. It felt like he had won the proverbial lottery. Gianna must have participated in the auction. Did her anger stem from having lost the bidding war?

The door to the festive salon opened. The ladies of the house had arrived.

Carlotta had parted from Peter with a very courteous gesture suggesting kisses flung about, leaving him alone in Ms. Jana's surreal old-modern office. He smoothed out his suit, still a little rumpled, and widened his tie half an inch. Glancing at the tie's subtle, chic pattern, he laughed softly. One benefit of the constant pressure of having to be Luisa's boyfriend was the fine clothing he owned. While he valued cleanliness and order, he didn't care for the latest fashions that reinvented themselves daily. Peter was content with the ever-changing demands of the online world. Luisa's demands had forced him to buy a series of expensive, exquisitely tailored suits. Today, his smile widening, he was for the first time actually benefiting from it.

Peter looked out the tall transom window into the torchlit garden. Two women in formal clothes were strolling, and the shadow of an upraised arm danced through the light cast on the lawn by the windows below. It had been a successful evening for the ladies of the house.

"Padrona Gianna," Selina said exuberantly, her red dress rustling as she moved toward the Italian. "I hope the comforts of the house may console you."

Gianna put her head back, laughing. "They already have," she said, spreading her toes. Michael didn't need to hear a command, and with a sigh, took them into his mouth, starting at the big toe.

Selina brushed his head. "Sweet Michael is here for a beginner's class," she said with a smile.

Gianna bit her tongue. "Oh, well, he already pampers feet like a pro. A little too selfish, but passionate."

Selina pulled on Michael's ear admonishingly. "You've received a compliment, slave."

With a grateful, loud smack, he released Gianna's big toe from his mouth. "Thank you, Padrona Gianna." The two ladies grinned at each other.

"A darling," Gianna judged, placing her feet one on top of the other. Michael licked her soles instantly, trying hard to put as much force into his tongue as possible. "He can't be older than 19, can he?" she asked, watching her foot licker's head bob up and down intently.

"Just 18," Selina whispered, "Or he wouldn't be allowed to be here. You should have witnessed him as a living instrument – a natural at devotion."

Gianna nodded, impressed. "I'll take your word for that."

The thumping of heels sounded in the hallway. Peter listened, still looking into the dark garden, immersed in dancing light from the torches. Ms. Jana entered her office. Peter turned away from the window after a deep breath and smiled. "Good evening."

The mistress of the house, wearing her high-necked ball gown, returned his smile. "Good evening, Mr. Wartmann."

They approached each other until they met in the middle of the large room, next to the flat coffee table and the white seating shells in which they had been brainstorming over Peter's important keywords together. Jana's eyes shone, her hair emphasizing the subtle movements of her head, as if it inhabited its own microcosm, where gravity was lower than on Earth.

Peter caught himself staring downright into her eyes and cleared his throat apologetically. "I am… blown away by the auction I had the pleasure of observing. I want to express my gratitude for the experience and my congratulations on the large sum."

Jana nodded sublimely. "Thank you. If it were up to my staff, the money has already been invested in new toys, a renovation of the basement, and a fleet of midnight black limousines. The women don't see" – Jana leaned forward, and the two could have kissed – "that it cost almost as much to train a slave of Fourteen's caliber and retain him during the long period when no lady was good enough for us or him."

Peter gulped.

Jana nodded imperceptibly. "The house is making profit. But that's because I have highly qualified servants who work without pay as electricians, janitors, stage and sound technicians, lifeguards, and gardeners." Jana snickered smugly.

"Working for you is the wage," Peter noted.

Jana shook her head. "Working for any of the ladies is. Most of the servants feel they belong to one of my ladies. Who would you choose," Jana asked unexpectedly, "if you could? You have met the inner circle of my most important employees today."

He opened his mouth, formed a sound, but only croaked softly. She tilted her head curiously. Silence. Peter waited for a redeeming laugh, a buddy-like hand on his shoulder that would relieve him of this question. Maybe even a wink, laced with a playful fist bump and a "Just kidding, Mr. Wartmann! Don't worry, we're business partners after all." His thoughts raced. He did not delude himself into thinking he had come here only out of erotic fascination.

Ms. Jana caressed his face. "You wear Carlotta's lipstick proudly," she noted.

Peter abruptly touched his cheek.

"Do you still think you're here for altruistic reasons?"

He shook his head, a hand at his face, his eyes widening.

Ms. Jana took another step closer. "Peter Wartmann, mere visitor at the infamous house?"

His head shake intensified. "No," he finally articulated softly. "I'm here because I want this house to have a great website." Jana smiled challengingly. That explanation was not nearly enough. "I've been so fascinated by everything here," he confessed. "By your lifestyle, by the things you've said. Since" – he sighed wearily – "since I met you, my life has improved. I've become braver. Happier. I want you to have a… a really awesome website that you're delighted with. One that works, one that attracts just the right men that you make your products from. I…" The essence of his motivation dripped from his lips and fell past Ms. Jana's dark blue evening gown, down to her beautiful feet. "I want you to be happy about me."

"Soooon…" Selina implored, her arms raised in excitement, "Just a few more seconds." The ladies of the house and their international guests, after enjoying a few bottles of champagne – and significantly stronger drinks – had discovered the ballroom's large hi-fi system to their liking. Lady Mei Ren, the Asian lady who first left the auction, sat on the large central couch. The bare buttocks of several slaves crouching on the floor stretched toward her, trembling. In her hands were two cream-colored pumps, the heels of which she clutched like drumsticks.

The moment everyone was anxiously waiting for was the famous onset of the throbbing drums that signified the catchier second part of Phil Collins' 'In the air tonight.' The Asian woman sat on the couch with her pumps raised to strike. Slave buttocks quivered beneath her gaze, as focused as it was menacing. Phil Collins' voice dropped out for the famous, impactful artistic pause before the drums kicked in, and Selina let her arm descend. "Now!"

Lady Ren yelled, hitting the buttocks in front of her so hard that her hairdo burst. She didn't hit a single note, but the ballroom screeched, "I can feel it coming in the air tonight, oh looooord!"

Ms. Jana smiled tenderly. "I *am* happy about you." Peter sighed, and a lump formed in his throat. "I am thrilled with your clever mind. I get furious when you launch into an explanation and then break off on your own, as if someone had said, 'Hey man, no one cares.'"

He looked into her beautiful face, and her amber eyes caught his, her softly swaying hair flowing around her delicate, yet sharply cut features. His heart beat up to his throat. "I know which lady of the house I would choose. And I've known it since our first meeting."

Ms. Jana impulsively put her arms around him, and he returned the gesture with vigor. She laughed affectionately at his enthusiasm, and he felt the vibration of her warm voice on his chest. As they let go of each other, she brushed his chin. "You've come to the right place."

Michael didn't know whether he should consider himself lucky or pity himself. His butt was burning from the blows of the Asian lady's pumps, but in return, Lady Janice had just freed him from his pink penis cage.

"I bet ya hope I lose it," she purred, slurring a little, raising the delicate key in front of his face. "Two more glasses of this, and I guarantee nothing."

Freed from all restraints, his penis straightened at the sight of the many ladies with pretty, bare feet, stilettos, pumps, and flamboyantly revealing evening attire. He could have marveled at his own lack of inhibition, the absence of any shame, but Carlotta, shoving her black high heels in his face and grinning broadly as she forced him to take a breath, demanded his full attention. Her dainty feet smelled of almost nothing. Her gesture, the audience, his nakedness, defenselessness, and the hint of skin cream he perceived made his cock grow to its full modest size.

"Stand up," the blonde ordered, positioning the lanky slave against the wall, wide legged. She tied his hands to two lamps and took several steps back, contemplating her handiwork.

The audience wrinkled their noses. "Dick too small," the Asian lady complained vehemently.

Gianna diMesa crossed her arms. "I thought it was the cage, but it really is a mini dick, girls." Laughter erupted.

Selina stepped forward and fondled Michael's chest. "Ladies, please! That's just the challenge."

Derya seconded, "I'll go first, but don't be outright intimidated if I hit a bull's-eye."

A defiant "Oooh" rippled through the tipsy group of women. Michael had no idea what the mistresses were up to. Derya took off her left shoe, weighed it in her hand, and swung out. He understood within a heartbeat what was going to happen – the thrown shoe was going to catch on his hard-on. Whether the heel and sole would wrap around the shaft and remain there, as in horseshoe throwing, or – as Derya was aiming for – one of the straps would catch on his piece, it didn't matter. The maîtresse de cuisine threw her shoe very sensitively and landed a painful hit in Peter's most sensitive spot. He winced and hissed miserably. To make matters worse, the heel hit the top of his own foot as it bounced off his abdomen.

Cheers erupted. "Almost! Who's next?"

Ms. Jana's hand slid from his chin downward. Peter took a deep breath. She smiled sweetly. "Nervous, Peter?"

He nodded.

Jana shook her head indulgently. "There's no need for that." She grabbed his tie and widened the knot with a gentle tug. "You keep that on. It matches your eyes." Peter raised his brows. Jana simply smiled. With a clearing of his throat, he slipped off his jacket, looking into her face as rigidly as he did uncertainly. She just kept looking back at him out of her surreal hazel eyes. He held his jacket in one hand and, for a brief moment, he looked around insecurely, as if searching for a place to put it.

She watched him. Peter didn't dare simply walk over to the table, so he gently dropped the bundle on the floor. His hand went to his top shirt button and paused briefly. The tie would hinder his undressing. Jana's eyes traveled downward, giving a hint. Peter mumbled understandingly and reached for the button of his pants instead.

"Legs wider," Selina demanded, and Michael obeyed with trembling knees. She took several swings and threw one of her red stilettos. By now, there were seven pretty shoes on the dark brown parquet floor in front of Michael. None of the ladies had yet managed to get one of them caught on his hard cock. Selina's shoe made a nice curve, thumped against Michael's belly and fell down, accompanied by an "Ooh!" from the ladies.

The idea of simply throwing the shoe against Michael's body and then hoping that one of the straps would get tangled on his cock as it fell down was innovative. Unfortunately, this attempt didn't succeed either, and Michael stared almost apologetically at the eighth shoe below him. Selina snorted in annoyance.

"Some aiming juice, my dear?" Janice asked, offering her a glass.

Peter's pants, shoes, and socks lay at his feet, and he emerged from the soft fabric with an unsteady step to the side. Jana looked at him patiently. She enjoyed this little humiliating ceremony. He had fetched his smartphone out of his pocket before dropping his pants and now stood in front of her in delicious insecurity. Jana clicked her tongue and kindly took it from him so he could take off his shirt. Her attentive gaze followed his fingers, trailing down from the collar lapel. He slipped off the white shirt, and she registered his tediously tucked in white undergarment with a wink. He pulled it over his head, almost taking his tie off with it. With a quiet smile, he looked at Ms. Jana. Wearing only his underpants.

She opened her hands. "Peter?"

He swallowed. "Ms. Jana?"

She smiled amiably at his cute uncertainty. "Please undress completely," she demanded, tilting her head with a broad smile.

He cleared his throat. "Ms. Jana, are we… Are you really interested in me in *this way?* I find" – he took a deep breath – "I find you extremely attractive, but we're crossing a line here. Yeah," he quickly added when she had opened her mouth, "I know that everything here – this house, your work, and my contribution to it – crosses lines per se. But I'm not sure—"

She interrupted, "You still think you're a normal man, don't you?"

Peter opened his mouth but couldn't get a word out for

the second time. Ms. Jana stroked his shoulders with warm hands, said "please follow me," and led him to her desk. She sat down in the office chair. He stood beside it a little lost. "Keep your undies on," she purred with a wink, "until I order them off one last time. Now sit down."

He looked at her in astonishment. No chairs in front of the desk. Then he turned his head toward the seating area in the center of the large office. A little too far away for an intimate conversation.

Ms. Jana crossed her legs and sighed sweetly. "On the floor, honey."

Wearing only his underpants, Peter sat down in front of Ms. Jana. She watched him as he slowly sank down and nodded when he reached his definitive position. "Great," she praised, caressing his head. Her crossed legs peeled seductively from the long slit of the dark dress. One of her feet hovered directly in front of him in its subtly glittering high heel. He managed not to let the small peek at her pretty, slender foot get to him. Or so he thought.

Ms. Jana sighed. "The best little SEO guy far and wide," she purred, her hand caressing his cheek. "So unhappily in love with a vicious woman because she tolerated his sexuality a little. Surpassing his colleagues in competence and overrules his superior in deciding to help my ladies and me. Alone, without his agency. Who, after one small compliment, goes out of his comfort zone and confronts his demoness at home, promptly bringing about the overdue end of the relationship." She leaned forward and smiled down at him. "Notice anything?"

"Are you," he whispered, "suggesting something like *fate*?"

Jana put her head back in sympathy-laden frustration. "Argh, Peter!" she scolded in amusement, tossing her head forward again so that her hair seemed to literally shoot out at him for a brief moment. "It speaks volumes about your wonderful character, your gentle soul, that you want to help me, that you sit here full of zeal looking up words for the search engine for entire evenings, not giving a single thought to the real why."

Peter frowned. "Yes, I have," he said quietly. "I have. After all, we established earlier that I'm here because I want you to be happy about me. Because I'm… sort of the submissive type, too, who might as well be a servant here. Maybe" – the perspective of sitting on the floor in front of her and looking up past her slender legs had loosened his tongue – "maybe I'd be ideal as something like your 'web slave,' or whatever you'd call it."

She smiled down at him and shook her head indulgently. "Take off your underpants." He was puzzled. She tapped her foot impatiently. "I won't repeat myself." She had changed neither volume nor intonation, but her words had acquired a startling sharpness that couldn't actually be there. Peter Wartmann took off his underpants. Ms. Jana nodded with a quiet smile.

"What…" he asked, realizing his voice was shaking, "do you think is the real *why* – the real reason I'm here?"

Jana watched as he sat back down at her feet. She sighed with affection for the stark naked Peter, who looked up at her with puppy eyes, so far from any field in which he was confident and self-assured. She cursed every person who had ever hurt this dear man, who was as happy as a child to find a good keyword, who put little pictures on websites and reported ideas to her in the manner of an eager student, proud of his findings. Jana gritted her teeth to avoid showing that her chin was trembling with anger and a tear was in her eye. "Because, Peter," she said, "You are a prime example of our non-failed existences. You're not just a submissive man. You're the raw material. Just as Fourteen once was."

His eyes widened. He opened his mouth to respond that she was mistaken. She had had this conversation a hundred times in her own head and knew every argument that did not come out of his mouth. Quite as expected.

It took Peter ten quiet minutes to fight a ferocious

battle in his own mind, him against himself. And Jana didn't make the mistake of touching him or saying anything now. His cheeks reddened and paled again. His mouth moved as if he were speaking. His eyes stared off into infinity. She was looking at him. When the battle ended in Peter Wartmann, he turned his head. Whatever would happen now, it marked an end and a beginning. Whether he agreed with her or decided to leave – Peter Wartmann was no longer the same. He did not speak, but slowly, with determination, raised his hands.

She nodded with a smile and turned her foot so he may touch it. Peter caressed her ankle, touched her toes, and slid a finger along her heel with well-measured force, without tickling her. Jana looked at him with tenderness. Peter touched Jana's pretty foot in her beautiful shoe adorned with wondrously ornate straps. More than mere touching with his hands would happen soon, he was sure, but the time had not yet come to think of such trivial things as kissing or licking her feet. He carefully touched each of her toes, and a soft, compelling smile, intriguingly reminiscent of the high after a joint, slipped onto his face. He bathed in his fetish. Ms. Jana bestowed upon him every touch he wanted to take. Peter placed the palm of his hand around her heel and heard his blood rushing into his head. She playfully lifted her toes and wiggled them twice. He laughed happily and looked up at her.

What he discovered there, however, was not the beautiful face of the mistress of the house, but the screen of his smartphone and the perplexed face of his ex-girlfriend, who had answered a late-night video call from his number.

She wasn't even muted. She had picked up the phone and immediately fell silent when she saw Peter. He must have been a sight to behold: naked except for his tie, on the floor of a stranger's house, one long leg hovering over his lap, which he touched and stroked as if befuddled with happiness. He looked Luisa in the eyes.

She shook her head. "Congratulations, Peter." For a moment, something like a defeated, completely flattened smile slid onto her face. "That's the last thing I would have expected from someone like you. Really, it's…" – she actually snorted – "that's like… the most severe middle finger you could have given me." He was completely speechless. "That's where you belong," Luisa decided, raising her hands in a gesture, as relieved as she was powerless. "What can I say? *Respect* for that? I wouldn't have expected it. Whatever you're doing seems to be doing you good." Another baffled snort ensued. "God, you really are the only man to grow a spine from kneeling down and shuffling about, aren't you? Anyway, wish you all the best. Thanks for making it so clear." And she hung up.

Jana put the smartphone down on her desk and looked at Peter, who was massaging her foot, lost in thought. He stared upward with a blank expression, to where the smartphone had hovered in her hand until a second ago. She had taken a risk, but little Luisa had reacted as expected.

Peter turned his head, and Jana thought she recognized the enthusiastic gleam in his eyes that he usually possessed only when he spoke of his work. She smiled. He was already beginning to tie the many loose threads in his head together. He was going to be a great product.

"Because…" he whispered, and she leaned forward, "Because sometimes freedom calls for chains." The truth of this banal paradox filled this strange moment with meaning.

Jana brushed his head. "It does, slave."

EPILOGUE 1: PER ASPERA AD ASTRA

The marble entrance hall was flooded with light. The ladies of the house stood in a semicircle opposite the wooden portal. A well-dressed man walked into their midst with measured steps. He proudly held his head. His light blond hair almost glowed in the sunlight that fell on him through the high windows. His young body was strong, though the word "muscular" would be a stretch. His back was straight, and in the curious movements of his head was no fear, but wholesome curiosity and anticipation.

A motor noise sounded in the driveway, grew louder, and finally faded out, seconded by the crunch of gravel in front of the large staircase. A car door thumped, and friendly voices greeted each other. The clatter of heels on stone steps sounded. The portal opened with an agonized squeak. Jana smiled.

Lady Elaine was a small young woman with wide hips and a sweet, round face. She wore jeans, low-heeled black shoes, and a lovely, colorful blouse. She spotted Michael in the middle of the hall, surrounded by the lionesses in whose den she had thrown him, and stopped abruptly.

Jana's smile widened. Lady Elaine had given the house a trembling youngling and was returned a young man brimming with strength and confidence, cultural education, and sexual hunger. She touched her face in astonishment at the sight of Michael.

"Get your slow butt over there," Janice hissed, and the ladies laughed as he started to move with his head humorously bowed and embraced his Elaine.

"You look great," she whispered, stroking his clothes.

Jana folded her arms in front of her lap. Selina discreetly glanced over at her, and Jana nodded in affirmation.

As expected.

The ladies had spoken often about little Michael as they noted and assessed his progress. Janice, Tatjana, and most of the others needed no particular mental intimacy with the temporary slaves who populated their day-to-day work. Selina, on the other hand, did. She had remarked to her superior several times that she suspected no real mistress behind Michael's owner, but rather a girlfriend bent on specific erotica. His strange mixture of prior knowledge of exotic practices, combined with worrying ignorance of a number of other things – including his safety during the performance of certain games – had given rise to this suspicion.

"As they say in science," whispered Carlotta, who had enough people skills to draw the right conclusions at the sight of the smooching couple, "Even negative results contribute to research."

Jana put an arm around her youngest employee with a grin. "It's not a negative result if he's all over her tonight and makes her realize that she really doesn't want to be a mistress, but his girlfriend. Look at how she's beaming. She certainly deserves the lovely man we have made of her pimple-faced toddler. Whether they maintain their lifestyle is not important to us. It's about love."

EPILOGUE 2: E.A.T.

"…as can be seen here in the illustration. The ladies will be amused to learn that the principle by which the largest and most famous search engine – Ah! – evaluates and displays our content can be abbreviated as E.A.T. Anyway, what I want to say is that E.A.T. stands for expertise, authoritativeness, and trust. A website that is capable of encompassing these three aspects will show up far – Ow! – in the search results. I assume I do not need to emphasize that these principles are not unlike our lifestyle in the house. Let's not get deeply philosophical and draw any conclusions from the perceived dominance of the – Mmmrgh! – search engines in our day-to-day lives to the reality of our sexuality. Nevertheless—"

Janice drew on her cigarette holder, and due to the poorly fitted filter atop, an almost inaudible, yet enervating whistling sounded as the smoke swirled through the slender ebony shaft. Jana raised her eyes. She had not prohibited smoking in the great conference room, yet they all knew she disapproved.

Janice noticed the irritated silence that fell. "Nemesis," she cursed, sticking the cigarette deeper into the holder.

With a mild smile, Jana turned her attention to the

lower end of the long conference table, where a stark naked man stood, a pink collar wrapped around his neck, the silver chain hanging down in front of his belly. Carlotta held its end in one hand and looked proudly at the trembling speaker. Her other hand caressed his exposed testicles, her touch as threatening as it was careless, suddenly squeezing now and then, just as she liked. The speaker nervously nestled the small remote control he used to switch between slides in his presentation between his fingers.

"Excuse the interruption, Cookie," Jana hummed. "Please proceed."

AFTERCARE

Fetish is delightful. Playing together with forms of humiliation is awesome. Reading about fetish and gently dominant ladies and their slaves is glorious. But it is not reality. Do you *feel good?* I hope so. Because you are awesome. You look wonderfully relaxed sitting there, shaking your pretty head over these lines. "What kind of an epilogue is that?"

None at all.

It's the afterword of a session, when the toe-sucker and the owner of the toes-sucked sit grinning across from each other over a cup of coffee. I want to bring you down to earth, and at the same time, thank you for taking this journey into eroticism with my characters, my dear Emmanuel and me. Whether you identify with the submissive men or the naughty women in my works – in fact, no matter what you identify as – you are wonderful, worthy of protection, and deserving of all the love and affection in the way you love best.

I hope you'll keep reading.

Lala Idrisse

ABOUT THE AUTHOR

Imagine your partner and you lived in a relationship with a little bit of a kink. Dominant woman, submissive man with a very strong foot fetish. And not just sexually, but on a day-to-day basis – which is not to say that you are constantly cracking the whip or that every interaction has anything to do with your feet. Everything is just charmingly different with you. For friends, family, and colleagues, this is as irrelevant as it is virtually undetectable. Even with "normal" couples, the woman sometimes puts her foot down when it comes to choosing a vacation spot, a restaurant, and – rumor has it! – the frequency and nature of sexual intercourse.

Now your husband turns to you with a particular erotic fantasy. He wishes to entrust his thoughts to a strict therapist in role-play, who will analyze, reprimand, and punish him. *Why not*, you ask yourself. The white blouse and pencil skirt fit, an almost too clichéd small notepad and large glasses, over whose rim you cast lascivious glances at your "patient," are quickly assembled.

Your partner confesses a youthful crush on his teacher's feet. You scribble eagerly along, ask snappy questions, and grumble discontentedly about your "terribly perverted patient," whom you exorcise such nonsense from with the back of your hairbrush after the conversation. He reports fantasies about auctions, wicked vacations, the attractive neighbor, the children's illicitly handsome pediatrician, and many more characters, places, and play ideas. You write along.

At some point, the notes turn into the first short story. You post it in a fetish forum anonymously and receive great applause from the readers. Quite enthusiastic about the lovely comments, you write the second story from the notes that develop during role-play with your partner. The erotic antics of the "Madame Thérapeute" soon become the star of the fetish forum.

Two women contact you. They ask if you would like to compile your stories in small books and publish them. Of course, you already had this idea yourself, but your profession and an ethos that goes along with it prevent you from publishing the notes of your erotic therapy sessions. You are, in fact, a (sex) therapist for adolescents and couples. So you decline in response to the two ladies' question. If that came out! One can already see the headlines: "Youth therapist cashes in on fetish smut!" But the two women don't give up: "We're not talking about a publication in France, Madame."

I'm Lala Idrisse. *Medusa* is my fifth fetish book and the second one published in English. Thank you for reading.

If you enjoyed this naughty little foot fetish work, write a review or give it a rating. Fetish is fun, after all. Let's normalize it.

Imprint

Lala Idrisse

c/o Block Services

Stuttgarter Str. 106

70736 Fellbach

www.ingramcontent.com/pod-product-compliance
Lightning Source LLC
LaVergne TN
LVHW050543160826
845677LV00011B/2161

* 9 7 9 8 8 4 6 1 3 6 7 4 8 *